MW00583579

QUEEN OF BARRAKESCH

DELANEY DIAMOND

GARDEN AVENUE PRESS

Queen of Barrakesch by Delaney Diamond

Copyright © 2020, Delaney Diamond

Garden Avenue Press

Atlanta, Georgia

ISBN: 978-1-946302-16-8 (Ebook edition)

ISBN: 978-1-946302-17-5 (Paperback edition)

This book is a work of fiction. All names, characters, locations, and incidents are products of the author's imagination, or have been used fictitiously. Any resemblance to actual persons living or dead, locales, or events is entirely coincidental. No part of this e-book may be reproduced or shared by any electronic or mechanical means, including but not limited to printing, file sharing, and e-mail, without prior written permission from Delaney Diamond.

www.delaneydiamond.com

ACKNOWLEDGMENTS

A very big thank you to Ayesha, Aziz, and Noesha for allowing me, after I finished my research, to ask them numerous questions about Arab culture and the Muslim faith. I truly enjoyed working on *Queen of Barrakesch*, and it was that much more enjoyable because of all that I learned. Their feedback was beyond helpful, and I'm forever grateful to them for their patience and willingness to answer my questions.

ARABIC WORDS/PHRASES

Habibti (said to a woman) – my love

Habibi (said to a man) – my love

Hayati – my life

Rohi – my soul

Khali – uncle, specifically mother's brother

Baba – daddy

Ummi – mommy

Walidi – a formal, respectful way to say Father

Shukraan – Thank you

Nikah – the marriage contract the couple signs

Haram – means that something is forbidden in Islam

As-salamu alaikum (a common greeting) – Peace be unto you

Wa alaikum assalaam – And peace be unto you, too

Inshallah – God willing

Subhanallah – various meanings, including "God is perfect" or "Glory to God," said during times of personal trial or struggle to restore perspective

Inna lillahi wa inna ilayhi raji'un – We belong to God, and to him we shall return

1

Warm, arid wind tore across Wasim's face as he crouched over the white Arabian horse, riding without a saddle. He'd lost his *ghutra* half a mile back when the white headdress and the *agal* flew off his head and became a casualty of the speed of galloping hooves.

The air whipped erratically at his clothing as the heels of his bare feet pressed into the horse's ribs, encouraging her to go faster. She tore across the ground, kicking up dust and racing toward the finish line, past shrubs and bushes that whizzed by in a blur of green against the golden desert sands.

Though a competition, the race was one of the ways Wasim bonded with his large family, an ancient sport and form of entertainment that was part of their Arab heritage. His two half-brothers rode close behind him, one on either side, bearing down his neck. His other brothers were farther behind, younger and not as experienced and unable to match the speed of their older siblings. Nonetheless, the thundering hooves of his pursuers urged Wasim to maintain a fast and steady pace, victory almost within reach.

The group rushed onward with him leading the pack and

finally, with a cry of victory, he crossed the finish line drawn in the sand, sailing past the group of friends and family gathered to watch—huddled in groups or seated atop the roofs of their vehicles—with cameras trained on the racers. With their fists raised, cheers went up from the spectators, and Wasim grinned in satisfaction, pulling back on the reins to reduce the horse's speed. The slowdown continued as he rubbed and gently patted her neck to show his appreciation for her hard work and bringing him yet another victory.

"I can't believe you won again!" Akmal, one of his brothers, yelled from behind him.

Wasim chuckled and steered the horse into a U-turn. "You should be used to it by now," he said arrogantly.

His brother shook his head in disgust, and Wasim laughed even harder.

Guiding the horse into a trot, he lifted onto his bare feet on her back, standing upright and holding the reins. He received more cheers and congratulations as he made a victory lap around his friends, cousins, and the ten of his sixteen siblings in attendance. When he finished showboating, he jumped off the horse and handed off the reins to an aide. He received a few pats on the back as he made his way to the food that had been set up for their evening meal.

Wasim rinsed his hands and joined the men congregated together. The women and children huddled at tables nearby, and the bodyguards ate finger foods and drank standing up, ever vigilant in the protection of the royal family.

The servants had prepared a feast of roasted goat, fragrant rice, and other fixings sure to satisfy after the tough race. Wasim sat cross-legged on one of the colorful pillows on the ground before a low table filled with food and drinks and picked up a piece of pita bread. He scooped up some hummus and popped the morsel into his mouth.

"You're ruthless, Wasim. You could at least let one of your

brothers win one time." Farouk, his friend and the husband of his older sister, sat across from him and barely hid his amusement. He was a thin man with a narrow face and very tall, standing a full head above Wasim.

"And why would I do that?" Wasim lifted his cup, and a servant came over and filled it with water.

"Out of the kindness of your heart."

Wasim took several large gulps and then had the servant refill the cup. "And let them think I'm soft? No way. I have to keep them humble."

Akmal picked up a piece of goat meat with his fingers. "His arrogance knows no bounds," he muttered.

They didn't have the same mother, yet there was no doubt that they were related—with the same copper-brown eyes and strong features inherited from their father. But Akmal was clean-shaven and as their father often complained, wore his hair too long.

Wasim clapped his brother on the back. "I'm tired of all the flattery."

The men all chuckled, and then the conversation turned to lighter topics as they caught up on each other's lives. Farouk announced that Wasim's sister was pregnant with their second child. One of their cousin's sons was headed to the United States for college, but his mother was worried about all the reports of gun violence in the country.

They continued talking as the sun went down behind the dunes and the night air grew cooler. The servants set up torches around the encampment, and after some time, the conversation turned to more serious matters.

"How was your fact-finding trip?" one of Wasim's younger brothers asked.

"Worth it. I learned a lot."

He had spent the last two weeks in Dubai, Paris, and Cairo, talking to government officials and engineers about the rapid transit systems in their countries. Currently, Barrakesch only had public buses, but with traffic becoming a problem as the country's population grew rapidly and tourism increased, his father had expressed interest in a rail system to ease congestion.

"When are you going to give Father a full report?" Akmal asked.

"In a couple of days, when he gets back from his trip. In the meantime, I have some personal things to take care of," Wasim said vaguely. He didn't mention that included a visit to the woman who'd spent way too much time in his thoughts during the two weeks he'd been gone. Silence met his response, and to put off further questions, he added, "I'm waiting for a few of the figures regarding cost, but I'll have a full report soon."

"Makes sense," Farouk said.

Wasim glanced at his brother, who their father wanted to become more involved in the issues of transportation. "Akmal, will you be at the palace and able to attend?"

His younger brother nodded. "I'll be there, *Inshallah*. I'm interested to see what you learned and how it could help us."

"Good."

These periods with his family were extremely important to Wasim but became rarer as they all became more preoccupied with their own lives. He glanced up at the star-filled sky. One of his favorite times to be in the desert was at night, when the stars dotted the dark canvas that could be black one day or—depending on location and the time of year—shades of blue and rose another. The vastness of the universe never failed to amaze him, and he could almost believe that if he stretched out a hand he'd touch one of the tiny dots, though they were trillions of miles away.

Much as he loved the peaceful atmosphere, fatigue threatened to overtake him. He'd arrived back in the country only this morning, and after handling personal meetings, had attended the race. He hadn't had a chance to wind down yet and needed to rest.

Stifling a yawn, he rose from the pillow.

"Going to bed already, old man?" Farouk teased.

"I'm afraid so. The bed of this old man is calling."

Wasim said goodbye to everyone, stopping first to give his older sister a kiss and congratulate her on the new baby. Then he walked away from the large group to a Jeep on the edge of the encampment. Five bodyguards followed.

He climbed into the passenger seat and the driver took off. His security—two each in a vehicle—shadowed them toward the capital city of Kabatra. Once they left the desert, two motorcycles joined the procession by pulling in front of the vehicle Wasim rode in.

As the eldest son and heir to the throne, Wasim had been gifted his own palace at the age of twenty-five. It was located about twenty miles outside the capital and within full view of the Persian Gulf. The entire complex was an extravagant display of wealth, though it paled in comparison to The Grand White Palace where his family lived.

Wasim's home demonstrated his independence and ability to set up his own household. At thirty-one he was past the age when he was expected to marry, but he had no such inclinations. With his father as healthy as a purebred horse, he would not have to consider marriage and heirs for a long time to come. So he enjoyed himself and indulged in the luxuries that came from being a descendant of a centuries-old dynasty flush with immeasurable wealth, and outside of Barrakesch he discreetly enjoyed the women who allowed him to charm his way into their beds.

As they approached, large metal doors decorated in Islamic design connected to the walls that ran around the entire compound, opened and allowed them to roll through. Wasim was escorted to the door, and the security on the inside bowed briefly when he entered. The sound of trickling water filled the air from the fountain in the middle of the enormous foyer that boasted a three-story ceiling, arched doorways that led into other rooms and hallways, and marble tile floors trimmed in gold.

Once a day, an attendant placed fresh flowers inside the fountain. They floated in the gently moving water and perfumed the air with their floral scent.

An aide appeared, silently bowed, and then crouched before Wasim. He removed Wasim's sandals and replaced them with a pair of dark slippers before leaving as quietly as he came. Wasim was about to head upstairs when his personal secretary, Talibah, appeared.

He lifted his eyebrows in surprise. "*As-salamu alaikum,*" he greeted her. "What are you still doing up?"

Talibah was a few years younger than him, with golden-brown skin and sharp but friendly charcoal eyes. She wore hijab and a traditional black abaya. She'd been his personal secretary for over a year, after his previous secretary retired. There had been talk that she was too young and inexperienced to serve in such an important role, but her work ethic and loyalty had impressed him, and so far she had proven him right to give her the promotion.

"*Wa alaikum assalaam,* Prince Wasim," Talibah replied, dipping her head in respect. "I received a call from the secretary of His Excellency King Khalid. Your father will return to Barrakesch tomorrow and requests your presence the day after at The Grand White Palace at one o'clock. He has asked for a confirmation before eight a.m. tomorrow."

Wasim knew better than to ask why. When King Khalid requested your presence, you dropped everything and went to see him. If he needed anything specific, he would have included those instructions in the request.

"What if I had stayed out longer tonight?" Wasim asked.

"Then I would have waited up longer until you arrived, Prince."

Wasim hid his smile of approval. Yes, she was a great addition to his inner circle.

"Inform my father's secretary that I will be there promptly at one."

"Yes, Prince."

"Now go to bed, Talibah."

She allowed herself a faint smile and then bowed. "As you wish, Prince Wasim."

She turned away toward one of the arched doorways, and Wasim took the elevator to his apartment on the fourth level. When the cabin came to a halt, he stepped onto white carpet that ran all the way to the bulletproof windows on the other side that overlooked the property and the Gulf beyond.

Wasim waved away the aide that took a step in his direction and went to stand in front of the window. Below, his personal zoo included two lions and their new cub, two tigers, and the recent addition of a family of chimpanzees. He frowned, his gaze settling on the lions sleeping next to each other on the grass under one of the trees. But he didn't have an issue with the lions. He was frowning because of what Talibah had said.

His father knew he'd come to visit soon to share his findings from his trip overseas. So why request his presence sooner?

2

"You're not getting any younger," Benu said.

Seated at the vanity in her bedroom, chin resting on her palm, Imani rolled her eyes in response to her mother's chastisement. She'd had this conversation before, and not only with her mother. Her father had uttered similar words in the past. Her parents meant well, but the constant harassment about getting married wore on her nerves. Particularly since she had no intention of simply getting married for the sake of getting married. When she did, it would be for love.

"Don't roll your eyes at me," her mother said, though she couldn't actually see Imani.

"Mama, I know I'm not getting any younger, but I still have a lot of life to live, and I have a little more than a month left on my assignment here."

"And when your assignment is completed, and you return to Zamibia, you will settle down." Her mother's voice had firmed, and Imani straightened in the chair at her adamancy.

"What are you saying?" she asked.

Her mother cleared her throat. "You might as well know, but since yet another of your relationships recently ended, your father has picked a man we both think would be a suitable husband for you."

"What!" The situation was worse than she thought.

"Don't be too quick to hate the idea. He is a successful businessman from Ghana and a cousin of one of the members of The Most High Council. Financially, you're both in a good place and would be a good match."

"I don't care whose son he is. I'm not marrying him." She should choose her husband. He shouldn't be chosen for her.

"Imani Karunzika, watch your tone with me!" Her mother's voice cracked down the line with authority. "Your father is right. You have to watch your fiery temper. That mouth and attitude is going to get you into a lot of trouble."

Out of respect, Imani clamped her lips shut, but she was not pleased.

"Do not be so quick to dismiss the idea. Your father and I only want the best for you, and this is a very good man. At least give him a chance. Spend some time with him."

"I have someone I'm already interested in."

"The Senegalese man? He's not worthy of your station."

Imani had met Abdou on a trip to Senegal. They'd stayed in touch sporadically over the years, and with his gentle nature she thought he could be the perfect husband.

"Imani, are you there?"

"Yes, Mama."

Benu's voice softened. "Be open to the idea, okay? Love can come later, which is why it's so important that you are compatible in the first place. Arranged marriages have been practiced for centuries all over the world and many have done well. Look at your father and me. I will send you a photo of your potential suitor. He is very handsome."

Imani heard the smile in her mother's voice and became more annoyed. "What's his name?"

When her mother gave the name, she didn't need to see a

photo because she remembered him. He was certainly better off financially than Abdou—a filthy-rich, domineering forty-something-year-old who'd inherited his father's utility empire. Absolutely not.

"Baba said I could choose my own husband. We had an agreement. Besides, since the last fiasco, I've decided to take a break from men and concentrate on my work when I return to Zamibia."

Benu sighed dramatically. "You'll never find a husband if you're busy with international trade agreements, business deals, and women empowerment seminars. I'm proud of you—we both are—but you must consider your future. Your father is concerned."

"Is he also concerned about my brothers?" Imani asked in a saccharine-sweet voice.

"Did you know a woman is born with all the eggs she will ever have?" her mother asked, deftly ignoring the question. She often shared medical facts, as if to remind herself that at one time she had planned to become a doctor, before she dropped out of college and married Imani's father.

"Yes," Imani answered dully.

"We are born with millions of eggs but lose approximately 11,000 every month. Your brothers can have children at almost any age. You cannot. You're twenty-eight years old, my love. You need to find a husband and have some babies before you run out of eggs."

Imani rolled her eyes.

"Let us see where this will go, okay? Humor me. Can I send you a photo of Kwadzo?"

There was no way she'd marry her parents' choice. She wouldn't even entertain him. He would most certainly try to stifle her independence and curtail her work, and she'd be miserable in a marriage like that. "Yes, please, send a photo."

"Good. Let me know what you think so that I can pass on your thoughts to your father."

"Will you also pass on my thoughts about how I feel about him setting me up for marriage?"

"Imani..."

She sighed without making a sound. "I'll talk to you soon, Mama. Unfortunately, I have to go now because I have paperwork to take care of. I love you."

"All right, my dear. Have a good evening, and let me know what you think when you get the photo."

Imani disconnected the call and walked over to the window that overlooked the backyard of the two-story home she occupied as the Zamibian ambassador to Barrakesch. From here she could see the full lawn and the decorative tile around the swimming pool. She'd soon be gone and would miss this place. Though she returned to Zamibia from time to time, she had spent most of the past six years in Barrakesch—first as a graduate student and then as an ambassador.

Her phone pinged and she glanced down at it. Her mother had sent a photo of her intended. He *was* handsome. Older. Distinguished-looking, with dark brown skin, thick eyebrows, and high cheekbones.

She sent a message: *He's handsome.*

Benu: *I knew you would think so. I will tell your father the good news!*

Imani sighed heavily, feeling as if a herd of camels had been deposited on her shoulders. Her mother was right, there were many successful arranged marriages, but there were unhappy ones, as well. Particularly if the couples were mismatched.

She set down the phone and exited the bedroom. Earlier, the scent of cooking lamb signaled that dinner would soon be ready. She couldn't get enough of Barrakeschi cuisine, and at her request, the chef prepared Zamibian and Barrakeschi food equally. Her chef had his own *bzar* recipe—a blend of pepper, cardamom, nutmeg, coriander, and ginger—that made the lamb mouthwateringly delicious.

Walking down the hall, her feet tread on the beautiful burgundy and green rug that stretched along the middle of the solid wood floor. As she neared the top of the stairs, she heard feminine laughter which sounded like her house manager, a Filipina woman named Vilma. She listened closely and also heard the low murmurs of a male voice but couldn't pick out any words. Yet she knew that voice, and the skin on the back of her neck pricked with heat.

She looked down from the top of the stairs, and there was Crown Prince Wasim ibn Khalid al-Hassan talking to Vilma. His unexpected presence sent pleasure coursing through her veins.

The minute he lifted his gaze and saw her, he pressed a finger to his lips, indicating Vilma should be quiet. "Shh, the boss is here," he said ominously.

Imani placed her hands on her hips. "Very funny. Stop corrupting my housekeeper, please. What brings you by?"

"A special delivery. The approval on the next phase of the oil drilling project." He held up a folder in his right hand.

"You're running errands for the Ministry of Oil now?"

"Not at all, but I can't trust Minister Nair to do a proper review because the poor man has a crush on you, and I'm concerned he'll give you too much leeway."

"A crush? On me? You're being ridiculous. You don't trust your own minister."

"I don't trust you."

Imani smirked, taking the barb as a compliment.

"Not that I blame Minister Nair, but you have the poor man wrapped around your finger."

"You're giving me way too much credit."

"Hardly, but I have a vested interest in making sure this

project goes well because of all the money involved. And this way, I get to spend time with my favorite ambassador."

The corners of Vilma's mouth lifted into a little smile, and Imani shook her head as if Wasim were being ridiculous. Still, she blushed. He could be quite the charmer—which made him an excellent emissary when his father called on him to be his representative abroad. She would miss spending time with him when she left.

Imani started slowly down the staircase. "There you go, being all charming again. I'll take a look at the contract and then you can be on your way."

"Vilma told me we're having lamb tonight."

The closer Imani came to Wasim, the more her stomach tightened. "We? Lamb for me, not for you."

Hospitality was an important part of Barrakeschi culture. Since Wasim arrived around dinnertime, it was a given that he was invited to join her and it was understood that he would accept. Nonetheless, she liked to tease him and knew he'd play along.

"You wouldn't be so cruel as to not invite me for dinner. A guest in your home. A prince, no less." One eyebrow over his brilliant copper-brown eyes arched in question.

Imani stopped several steps above him. *Wasim.* In Arabic, his name meant "handsome" and "graceful." He was aptly named.

He wore traditional attire today, and from her position on the staircase she had the height advantage and a clear view of every angle in his handsome face beneath the *ghutra* that covered his head. The low, neatly trimmed beard couldn't hide the power of his square chin and jaw, nor could the white *dishdasha* obscure the width of his shoulders and the fitness of his firm body.

"There's only enough food for one. Sorry, you should have

told me you were coming." Imani shifted her gaze to Vilma. "We'll be working in my office."

"Yes, Ambassador."

Vilma walked away and Imani preceded Wasim down the hall. On either side were tan walls displaying paintings and photographs of ambassadors who'd lived there before her. "Your visit has really surprised me. I assumed you'd be spending time with your family." She glanced at him over her shoulder.

His gaze shifted from somewhere below her waistline to her eyes, and a moment of acknowledgement passed between them that heated her cheeks. The loose-fitting black abaya hid her body well, yet she felt unclothed before him. Jittery. Off. He'd always made her feel that way, and she fought those sensations by teasing and joking with him often. But in the past nine months, those sensation had become more pronounced—ever since their unexpected interaction the night of the polo match in Estoria last year.

"I was with my family and friends yesterday in the desert," he answered smoothly, seemingly unperturbed that she'd caught him looking where he had no business.

"Racing?"

"Yes."

"And did you win?" Imani opened the door to her office.

"I always win." He followed behind her and left the door open, per the custom when an unmarried woman and man were alone together.

"Such confidence."

Wasim chuckled and placed the folder on the table in the sitting area. He sat on the cream sofa and stretched an arm across its back, looking perfectly relaxed.

His commanding presence filled a room decorated in neutral colors with splashes of gold and silver. The pillows on the sofa were cream-colored and covered with gold and silver zigzagged lines. The rest of the office was bright and airy, with large windows on each side that she sometimes opened to let in cool air when the weather was pleasant. She did that now, pushing a window outward behind her desk and opening the French doors that led onto the patio.

Imani picked up her reading glasses from the desk—one of several she kept in various rooms around the house so she wouldn't have to remember to carry them with her at all times.

She walked over to where Wasim sat, feeling his eyes on her every movement. Annoyingly, her heart raced a little. Ever since she had met him through her cousin, Prince Kofi, Wasim had affected her. They had a playful relationship—teasing, flirting, even linking arms or the occasional touch—but outside of Barrakesch. Inside the country, that type of touching was forbidden in public between unmarried members of the opposite sex.

Wasim always shifted easily into the customs once they returned to Barrakesch, but for her, the transition was much harder. It frustrated her that she couldn't touch him, and that frustration highlighted the fact that her feelings were entering dangerous territory. Part of her wondered what would happen if she took his flirtations seriously and disclosed her feelings. Would he—no point in letting her thoughts go there. They were friends, nothing more. He was next in line to the throne of his country, and she would be leaving Barrakesch very soon.

Imani sat across from Wasim in a thick-cushioned armchair covered in cream and gold fabric and picked up the folder. She perused the document, the words he crossed out, and the comments in the margins. This was her biggest project to date, and one that she was especially proud of. To think, she would be a key player in taking her country's economy to the next level.

Zamibia had discovered oil off its shores in the Atlantic Ocean, and with help from Barrakesch, who had much more experience in offshore drilling than they did, intended to take advantage of this new means of income for their country.

Imani had been instrumental in arranging an exploratory agreement between the two countries, and she was now working on the final negotiations where they would create a joint venture to extract the oil. When the details were finalized, King Khalid—Wasim's father—and King Babatunde—her uncle in Zamibia—would sign the agreement.

Billions would pour into Zamibia and remain in the country to boost the economy. She'd already worked on a budget that used a small percentage of that revenue to fund her causes, all geared toward female empowerment through education and entrepreneurship.

Imani tossed the folder on the table. "Looks good so far. I expect to have the final analysis from the environmental commission soon, and then we'll be able to iron out a final deal." She could barely contain the excitement in her voice.

Wasim smiled. "I think that's cause for a celebration, don't you?"

"Before everything is finalized?"

"Absolutely. We're nearing the home stretch."

Imani cocked her head to the side. "What did you have in mind?"

"Oh, I don't know...stewed lamb?"

She giggled and shook her head. "Did you just invite yourself to dinner, Prince Wasim?"

"Yes, and you better say yes."

Though he was joking, his voice held an undertone of authority that spiked heat in her blood. "Well, with a command like that, how could I refuse?"

3

Once again, Imani's chef had outdone himself, and the hearty meal of stewed lamb over rice served with roasted vegetables was quickly consumed on the patio outside her home office.

She had a glass of wine with the meal, which she couldn't do in restaurants or anywhere else in the country because of the restrictions against the public consumption of alcohol. Wasim didn't consume alcohol at all, and instead had a glass of *jellab* in front of him—a drink made of grape molasses and rose water and garnished with pine nuts on top.

During the course of the meal, they discussed the oil drilling project in more detail and touched briefly on other government issues.

After the dishes were cleared away, Wasim poured them both a cup of tea. "Dinner was excellent, as always," he said.

"I'd be lost without my chef. You, however, have an entire team in your kitchen and yet, here you are, eating my food. It can't possibly taste better."

"On the contrary."

Imani arched an eyebrow.

"It's the company, you see," he explained.

"Oh yes. Because you're in the company of your favorite ambassador."

"Exactly," he said.

Imani shook her head as if disgusted, but he knew she enjoyed the compliment, even if she thought he was spewing out empty words. She was adorable and sexy and shared a similar sense of humor to him—an acerbic wit that sometimes had him chuckling to himself long after they'd parted ways because of something she'd said.

But the years since he'd known her had been challenging, to say the least. During this time he'd watched, being a friend, but craving her in a way he hadn't any other woman. No one knew the restraint he'd exhibited in the face of such temptation.

Lioness Abameha—the honorific bestowed on her by her uncle, the king of Zamibia—Imani Karunzika had come into his life six years ago when she attended the University of Barrakesch to earn a graduate degree in international business. Vivacious and funny, she had a certain determination that intrigued him. And she was a stunning woman with glowing bronze skin, sultry dark eyes fringed by thick lashes, and sexy curves that drew the eye and tempted him to touch. His first sight of her had sent his heart thumping.

But he'd known better than to give in to temptation. His good friend Kofi—her cousin and Crown Prince of Zamibia—had asked him to look out for her, even though she came with a set of bodyguards. They'd seen each other only a handful of times during that two-year period, until she was appointed ambassador to Barrakesch immediately upon graduation—one of the perks of being a member of the royal family. But she was good at her job and worked hard. Sometimes he thought too hard, as if something other than personal goals influenced her work ethic.

They saw each other more frequently once she became an ambassador. They attended many of the same official functions, and so their friendship blossomed and his attraction to her increased. No doubt in his mind that she knew her power over men. Her very bearing suggested that she did, and she wielded her beauty as one of the tools in her vast arsenal of weapons.

Outside of Barrakesch, she was brazen in the way she touched him, and he, too, initiated contact—torturing himself in ways that could only be deemed masochistic. Even he, with his ironclad will, could only handle her in small doses, so he pitied the fools who had crossed her path and been left scarred and broken by her personality and sensual allure.

"So, whose heart did you break while you were overseas?" Imani stirred honey into her tea.

"Me, a heartbreaker? I should be asking you that. I've lost track of your many boyfriends."

"Don't exaggerate. I've only been on a few dates in the past few months, and..."

"And...?" he prompted.

"Let's just say I've had to kiss a lot of toads in the quest to find a prince." She pressed her lips together.

"Well, if it's a prince you're looking for..." Wasim raised an eyebrow.

"You were never in contention," Imani said. She dislodged a strand of hair from her eyelash. Her hair was cut in a bob that made her thick, silky hair appear even thicker.

Wasim laughed softly and pressed his right hand against his heart. "I am crushed. Why? Because you refuse to take orders?"

"I may not be a princess, but I'm a member of the royal family of Zamibia, and not very good at taking orders," she said haughtily.

"I know. That's why I mentioned it. So tell me, what have

you been up to while I was gone? Skip the part where you tell me how much you missed me. I already know that."

"You are so conceited. No wonder you can't find a woman to marry you."

"And what's your excuse for remaining unmarried?"

"Ouch. For your information, it's rough out here for us women." She carefully sipped the tea, narrowing her dark eyes against the steam that wafted up from the colorful glass cup.

"From what I heard, it's rough for the men," Wasim said dryly.

"What have you heard?" she asked sharply.

"Aren't you the woman who punched your last suitor in the nose?"

Her eyes widened. "Who told you that?"

"Kofi."

"Oh. He hit me, so I hit him back." She shrugged.

Imani was the only female child in her family. Between her mother and her father's two other wives, she had six brothers. She'd learned to fight, including box, since she was young. Since she was a member of the Mbutu tribe, the fiercest and most warlike of the nine tribes of Zamibia, her ex should have known better. What did he think would happen when he put his hands on her?

Though she could take care of herself, if Wasim had been anywhere near, the man would have gotten much worse than a punch. Wasim would have put him in the hospital.

"You've always been very good at getting rid of the men in your life," he remarked.

"You make it sound like it was my fault," Imani said.

"Not at all. I find your ways to be very efficient. You don't waste time getting emotional about the decision. You do what needs to be done. Like the one before him—he cheated on you, did he not? And you dumped him right away instead of wallowing in nostalgia and listening to his excuses." He picked up his tea, which he'd completely forgotten about during their conversation. The minty, warm liquid coursed down his throat.

"There was no excuse for what he did. He had to go."

"And what about the one before that?" Wasim asked, setting the cup back on the table.

"Too weak."

"I see. And the one from Mozambique?"

She laughed. Such a lovely sound. "You know way too much about my love life, but to answer your question, we mutually agreed to split. We had no chemistry."

"Do you ever plan to get married?"

"Of course," Imani said.

"And what do you want in a man?"

They'd never had this type of conversation before, and he wasn't even sure why he'd taken it in this direction except that he wanted to know more about her needs and wants. A certain restlessness had pervaded him of late, and she was at the center of it.

"Planning to set me up with someone?" Imani asked.

"Depends on what your answer is. I have to be considerate of my friends."

She shot him a dark look, and he stifled a laugh.

Imani surveyed the property for a bit, seeming to really think about her answer. "I want a man who is smart, funny, good-looking, but he doesn't have to be a head-turner. He should be good with children, too, and..."

"Able to handle you?" Wasim supplied.

"I don't have such lofty expectations. There's not a man alive who can handle me."

He let loose his laughter this time.

She smirked. "And you? What are you looking for in a future wife?"

"I'm not looking for a wife."

"You will eventually. You are, after all, the oldest son of King

Khalid. Eventually you'll be king and you'll need heirs. You're not getting any younger, so what's the delay?"

He didn't have an answer. He didn't know why he had delayed for so long except that the women he'd met over the years didn't measure up, and as each year passed, his father became more concerned about his unmarried status. He worried, too, about his antics abroad.

Wasim took advantage of his lack of notoriety outside of the Arab world. Though he always traveled with bodyguards, they were unobtrusive when he wasn't on official business, and dressed in Western clothes, he easily blended in.

He did activities like take public transportation and eat street food, the latter being a cause of great concern for his family and the aides traveling with him. But what was the point of being the son of a king if you couldn't enjoy what the world had to offer—both great and small? One day he wouldn't be able to take such trips, and until then, he intended to enjoy himself.

"I'll marry when I'm ready."

"And when you're ready, what will your princess look like?"

He sat back for a moment and seriously considered the question. "She must be funny, intelligent, and able to carry on a good conversation. Knowledgeable about politics and world events, and she must be able to handle me."

"Hmm, that poor woman."

"Obedient."

Startled, Imani repeated, "Obedient?"

He was kidding, but her expression was amusing. "This is my fantasy wife, remember? Can I finish?"

She gestured with a hand for him to proceed.

"Compassionate and like your ideal man, good with children. Someone who can play and laugh with them."

"I assume you're finished now?" Imani asked.

"And obedient."

"You said that already."

"It's worth repeating because it's very important."

She narrowed her eyes at him.

Wasim pretended not to notice her glare and tapped his middle finger on the table. "Let's see...I think that's it for now."

"Good luck finding that fantasy," Imani muttered.

"Good luck finding yours."

"I don't need luck. I'll simply be patient."

"I'm sure your patience will pay off. There are many men looking for a woman like you—intelligent, strong-willed, and sure in her convictions."

"You think so? Women like me have a hard time finding a good man."

"Perhaps women like you are looking in the wrong place." His answer forced her into silence, and she studied him across the table. "But you don't have anyone in mind right now?"

She shifted in the chair. "Not since the last fiasco, but my parents are now talking about an arranged marriage."

Wasim froze, body going perfectly still. "When did that happen?"

She lifted one shoulder dismissively. "The option has always been on the table, particularly where my father is concerned, but I've told them I'm not interested in them setting me up."

"Why not?"

"Like I told you before, that's the old way. I want to find my own husband. I want to be in love when I marry."

"And that's part of the fantasy?" Wasim asked.

"Falling in love is not a fantasy."

"Don't you believe that two people can be happily married even if they're not in love? Both of us have parents whose marriages were arranged. It's not necessary to love first if you're compatible."

"For me it is. Otherwise, the marriage is more like a business arrangement, and I couldn't be happy in a relationship like that." She wrinkled her nose. "Besides, I think I've found a man already."

The tightness in his body increased. "You have? You just said there was no one."

"There is."

"And you're in love with him?"

"I like him and believe I could come to love him once we start dating. He's a businessman from Senegal. We met a while back."

"I vaguely remember you telling me about him. Abdou something, isn't it? He's not worthy of a woman like you," he said gruffly.

"Well, lucky for me, you don't get to choose my husband."

Despite their commonalities, they also had many differences between them. Imani was Christian, he was Muslim. Her permanent home was in Africa and his in the Middle East. Now, another one. Where she believed falling love was integral to a happy marriage, he didn't hold the same belief.

That thought unsettled him deeply, but rather than voice his opinion, he remained quiet and took another sip of tea.

4

In the back of a limousine on the way to The Grand White Palace, Wasim reviewed his notes in preparation for the meeting with his father. The final figures had come in last night, and he'd plugged them into the spreadsheets and had Talibah print copies of the report for him, his father, and Akmal.

Under normal circumstances, the reviews would be done via electronic tablets, but his father was old-fashioned and preferred to have the weight of papers in his hands. Wasim had been very impressed with Cairo Metro, the first constructed rapid transit system in the Arab world. He'd also learned quite a bit in Dubai and especially Paris, whose extensive system of lines and stations was one of the oldest in the world.

His attention was drawn outside the window to a red tour bus rolling along the highway, a reminder that tourism revenues had become a larger line item in their budget in recent years—the very reason they were exploring expanding public transportation.

Having more people come to the country was a good thing. From experience, he knew that outsiders mistook their traditional dress and codes of conduct as an indication that they were a backward nation. They expected to see camels and souks and horse-drawn carts. While those existed in some of the older areas, where the ancient streets were narrow and the Ministry of Historical Preservation maintained the authenticity of relics from the past, the country was crisscrossed by modern highways and glass skyscrapers. Throughout Barrakesch, ancient and modern coexisted.

The limo cruised to a stop at the checkpoint with armed guards dressed in military gear before driving another two miles down a winding road with palm trees on each side. At the end of the road, the splendor of the palace loomed before him.

Consisting of six floors with hidden passageways, elevators, and grandiose designs that included imported marble and decorative touches trimmed in gold, The Grand White Palace was located in Kabatra and a short distance from the city's harbor.

Heavily guarded, the palace was a symbol of wealth, as well as paid homage to the region's aesthetic. The large doors at the entrance were designed in typical Islamic architecture with the family emblem of a resting falcon at the top. As of five years ago, on Mondays and Wednesdays visitors could tour sections of the compound and inside the palace.

The Grand White Palace was not only the home of King Khalid, his two wives and their children and their children, but where several government offices were located, including an office where Wasim sometimes worked. The king also met with his advisors there, and once a month citizens could come to plead their cases to the king in The Great Hall of Appeals— asking for leniency on prison terms on behalf of loved ones, economic relief, to settle land and business disputes, or other matters of importance.

Wasim's older sister, Yasmin, was exiting with her four-year-old son as he entered through one of the side doors. She wore her raven hair cascading down her back, black slacks, and a long-sleeved blouse whose coral color complimented her skin tone.

"*Khali!*" his nephew said, his eyes brightening.

"And where are you going?" Wasim asked, lifting his nephew, Malak, into the air.

The little boy giggled. "Me and *Ummi* are going to meet *Baba* for lunch."

"Sounds like fun. Bring me back some *kanafeh*, okay? I haven't had any in a while."

"Okay!" his nephew said with an enthusiastic grin.

He kissed Malak on the cheek before setting him on the ground.

"Going to see Father?" Yasmin asked.

"Yes. He, Akmal, and I are going to review the reports from my trip." He held up the folder that had been wrinkled a bit when he lifted Malak. "What's the occasion for lunch?" he asked.

"Farouk and I have a meeting downtown about one of his latest projects, but he's taking us to lunch first. I'll take Malak to a friend's while we're in the meeting."

Farouk always included Yasmin in his business dealings, trusting her judgment and ability to read people. His construction company had been modestly successful when he met her, but since marrying, the business had grown by double digits every year. Partly because of his connections to the royal family, but also because of Yasmin's input.

"And which project is this?"

"The new Hilton Hotel on the other side of town."

He knew that project. It was a huge undertaking—easily the biggest of Farouk's career. No wonder he wanted Yasmin present.

"And look what he bought me." She tucked her hair behind her left ear and showed off the diamond stud.

Wasim whistled. "Very nice. What's the occasion?"

She shrugged, a blush of pleasure on her cheeks. "No reason. Just because."

He almost wanted to call Imani and say *See, here is another arranged marriage that's working just fine.*

"He spoils you too much," Wasim teased.

"There is no such thing," Yasmin said loftily. "You could never be too good to a woman. Remember that." She strutted across the tiled courtyard toward the vehicle idling nearby. Malak waved goodbye and Wasim waved back.

They disappeared within the Lexus SUV, and Wasim entered the building. One of the staff handed him a wet towel that he dabbed against his face to cool off from the heat. Then he took the elevator to the top floor and entered his father's quarters. There, an aide removed his sandals and replaced them with a pair of slippers. He escorted Wasim toward the glass-enclosed balcony where his father sat in a chair covered in gold and oxblood fabric.

He didn't announce his presence, and King Khalid didn't notice he had arrived. The older man stared out at the water, which at this time of the day, with the sun high in the sky, glinted like diamonds had been scattered across its surface.

Wasim noted with a bit of alarm that his father's robes hung more loosely on him, an indication that he'd lost more weight. He would need to have a stern talk with him about this vegan diet he'd adopted. *For health reasons,* he'd said, but Wasim didn't like the rapid weight loss. He and Yasmin had discussed their father's appearance once before, and he'd bring it to her attention again so they could address the issue with him.

The king seemed to be focused on his yacht moored in the water, but Wasim suspected that he wasn't really looking at it. Under the *ghutra* and long beard peppered with gray, he seemed...aggrieved. The expression on his face pricked Wasim's heart, and he wondered if he was thinking about Wasim's mother again. The anniversary of her death would be in a few weeks.

King Khalid's second wife, her children, and staff resided on the fifth floor in the east wing. His third wife resided on the fourth floor in the east wing. He lived on the top floor in his own apartment, alone ever since his first wife, Wasim's mother, had tragically drowned. Twenty-six years had passed since her death.

At one time, Wasim had assumed his father had moved on. But after he hadn't moved either of his new wives into the queen's apartment on the sixth floor, he realized his father had not. His new wives had kept him from being lonely over the years, but they'd never replaced her in his heart.

He moved closer and his father glanced over at him, his face brightening.

"*As-salamu alaikum, Walidi.*" He bowed slightly.

"*Wa alaikum assalaam.*" King Khalid opened his arms, inviting him in for a hug.

Wasim embraced him, noting again the lack of bulk in his body since the last time he'd seen him. "You looked deep in thought."

King Khalid nodded. "I was. Thinking about a lot of things." His tone sounded rather serious—downright grave. He waved at the food spread out on the table between them. "Have something?"

Wasim shook his head. "I ate an early lunch, but I'll have a drink."

King Khalid called for one of the servants standing nearby, who immediately filled a glass with *jellab* and then stepped back, inconspicuous against the window.

Wasim sipped the cold drink in appreciation. Then he handed over one of the reports to his father. "Where is Akmal?"

"Running late, as usual," his father replied, pursing his lips in annoyance. "At least he called this time."

There was nothing his father hated more than tardiness, and Akmal seemed bound and determined to make his blood pressure spike by constantly showing up late to meetings and events. He was young—only twenty-five—but not too young to know better.

"Everything set for the technology expo in a couple of weeks?" his father asked.

"Yes. So far, so good. I'm convinced it's going to be a success."

This was a project he'd been planning for years—to have an expo that focused on technology—highlighting innovations in cybersecurity, high-tech, and robotics, and bringing together companies from the Arab world to create partnerships. But his vision had taken on a life of its own and become larger than expected, pulling international interest that expanded the attendees well beyond his expectations.

"Good. I won't be able to attend, but you don't need me there anyway, this is your project." King Khalid set aside the report. "Before we get started with that, I wanted to talk to you. Alone."

As he dismissed the servants hovering nearby, unease settled in the pit of Wasim's stomach. The other night when he'd gotten the message he'd immediately sensed that something was wrong but had brushed aside his concerns since then. Now they resurged anew.

When they were alone, his father looked at him, his expression so morose—so defeated—panic clutched at his abdomen.

"*Walidi*, what is it?" Fully focused, Wasim set aside his report.

"I don't know how to say this. I haven't gotten used to the idea myself."

The smile he gave Wasim wavered at the corners. Wasim couldn't smile back at all, and the sense of panic only increased, tightening to pain in his chest.

"I'm sick, Wasim. Very sick."

"Sick? How? What's wrong?"

"I'm in the advanced stages of pancreatic cancer."

What? Wasim's lips formed the question but never uttered the word aloud.

"I was diagnosed several months ago, and since then we— my doctors and I—have tried to find a way to make this go away through alternative treatments. I told them I do not want chemotherapy."

"That's why you changed your diet?"

He nodded. "I thought it would help. I was willing to try anything." He sighed heavily.

"Why didn't you tell us? Me, at least?"

"I didn't want to worry you, but the cancer is in the advanced stages. They don't give me much time."

Wasim shot from the chair. "No. There must be some mistake. We need a second opinion." He was ready to handle the situation. "We'll go to Dubai or Malaysia or Singapore. India! We could..."

The muscles in his throat constricted at the devastating thought of losing his father. He was already grief-stricken and his father hadn't passed yet. What would he do without him? What would this country do without him?

King Khalid's eyes bore the heaviness of sympathy, when in fact he was the one who needed sympathy. He clearly saw Wasim's fears.

"Sit, Wasim," he said wearily. "That's why I went abroad. To get a second opinion. But it's too late. Nothing can be done."

"How much time do we have?" He remained standing, forcing the question past stiff lips.

"A few weeks," his father said in a grave voice.

A few weeks! This couldn't be happening.

"That's why I wanted to talk to you privately. To tell you about my illness and a decision I've made. I want you to become the ruler of Barrakesch. I think you would be good for the country, but you don't have a wife."

"*Walidi...*" Wasim started with dread.

"Not even a prospect with the chance to start a family. You've turned down every potential wife your aunt has brought to you." Since Wasim's mother had passed, his father's sister was responsible for helping him choose a wife. "Before I die, I need to know I'm leaving the country in good hands, with a ruler who is stable and can provide an heir. Since you cannot provide the peace of mind that I—*we* need—I have made the difficult decision to choose someone else to succeed me."

Wasim sank onto the chair with the heaviness of a stone dropping to the bottom of the ocean. He hadn't expected to have to take the throne so soon, and he hadn't expected his father to pass him over, either.

"There are already factions in the Parliament who think you're too flamboyant, too reckless, and too progressive. With no wife and the possibility of continuing our line, their confidence will be further shaken and could result in unrest, upheaval in the government."

"That is ridiculous! You said yourself that I would be a good king."

"I have no doubt, but others have doubt. And a good king would make sure there is a clear line of succession in place. That is what I intend to do, and you would be required to do if you were king. I am sorry, Wasim. You've left me no choice."

"You have a choice. You could do what you know is right for the country, not what a few hard-headed conservatives want. The throne is mine. It is my birthright!"

"*Wasim.*" His father's voice took on an imperial tone, demanding respect. "The decision has been made. I will not change my mind."

Wasim stared at the tiled floor of the balcony, anger and

disappointment rolling in his blood. "When will you announce the successor?"

"In a week's time, when I announce my condition to the country."

"Who have you chosen?"

"I haven't made a final decision yet, but I will soon. Son, you won't be king, but I need your help over the next few weeks. There is much to do."

He was obligated to help. Not only because this man was his father and king, but because as a son and a subject, he wanted his father to go into the afterlife with his mind at ease. It would be his honor to do whatever he could to facilitate that transition.

With a heavy heart, Wasim took his father's hand. "What do you need me to do?"

5

Imani lifted herself out of the water and picked up one of the towels she had left poolside on a chair. She removed her swim cap and wrapped a towel around her wet hair and then proceeded to dry her body with the other towel.

Much of her days were spent in ceremonial tasks, handling visa requests, and negotiating agreements between businesses located in the two countries. Today had been particularly stressful because she'd been unable to get a reliable answer about the environmental report from anyone in the commission's office.

A relaxing swim had been exactly what she needed. Tomorrow she would begin the unpalatable task of trying to get an official report so they could make progress on the oil-drilling agreement.

She climbed the stairs to her bedroom and went into the large shower stall. She took a cool shower, washing her hair and skin thoroughly. After stepping out, she smoothed shea butter infused with the scent of passionfruit into her skin and pulled on a black abaya over a tank top and shorts.

Her personal aide, Doreen, who'd traveled with her from

Zamibia, came into the room as she finished getting dressed. The older woman was of medium height and thick, with light-brown skin and dark eyes. Imani sat in the chair before the mirror and Doreen blew out her thick hair. She made the strands bone-straight and then added fullness with a few twists of a large-barreled curling iron.

Imani examined the finished product. "Looks good. I feel like a new woman." She checked the profile view. The light use of argan oil gave her hair a silky and shiny appearance.

"You've been working too hard," Doreen said as she put away the oil and iron.

"I want to make sure the incoming ambassador has very little to worry about," Imani said.

"Well, they certainly won't."

The intercom phone rang and Doreen went over to the wall beside the bed and answered it. Seconds later, she turned to Imani. "Vilma says Prince Wasim is downstairs and would like to speak to you."

She hadn't been expecting him. "Tell her to take him to my office. I'll be right down."

Doreen nodded and repeated the message. When she left, Imani checked her face and applied lip gloss, which gave her mouth a hint of ruby color and a shimmery, moist appearance.

"Stop it," she muttered with a shake of her head. "It's just Wasim."

She exited the bedroom and went downstairs to the office and found him standing in front of the French doors. As usual, her stomach did that odd tightening motion whenever she saw him. He was dressed semi-casually today in a white long-sleeved shirt and black slacks, a combination he often wore. With one hand tucked into his pants pocket, he seemed to be at ease at first glance, but she knew him well enough to know he wasn't. Tension rested in his shoulders and rigid back.

"Hi, Wasim."

He turned, and his face confirmed her suspicions. Something in his eyes called to her. She sensed all was not well.

"I hope you don't mind that I popped up unannounced."

"I'm used to it," she said, softening the words with a smile.

"I say that every time, don't I?" He smiled back.

"Yes, you do. Can I help you with something?" She glanced around the room and didn't see any folders or paperwork.

"This is a personal visit," he explained.

"Oh."

"I called Kofi and Andres, but neither of them were available. So, you're in luck. You get to hear the news."

"I guess being third on your list isn't so bad," Imani said teasingly.

Wasim strolled over to one of the armchairs and sat down. Imani sat catty-corner to him on the sofa.

"What's wrong?" She'd never seen him like this.

A pained smile crossed his lips. "I don't know where to begin."

"Start where you feel comfortable."

Their friendship was such that they could segue into more serious matters even though they typically maintained an easygoing, teasing relationship.

With a wry twist of his mouth, Wasim said, "I had an interesting talk with my father. It seems not settling down has consequences."

"Oh." Keeping her voice light, Imani said, "Goodness, he's like my parents. There's no rush."

"On the contrary, there is a rush," he said grimly, ominously. "He's passing me over for the throne."

"What?" Imani's mouth fell open.

"You heard me correctly. There was a time when I didn't want the position, but in recent years I've changed my mind. There are plans I want to implement which I won't be able to unless I become king. The throne is *mine*. If I choose to decline it, that's a different matter, but to be passed over is…unacceptable."

The vehement tone of his voice and the way his eyebrows lowered over his eyes indicated his displeasure. Wasim played hard, but he worked hard, too, and she knew that one day he would be a good king.

The changes he wanted to make were unpopular ones his father had been unwilling to attempt. Among them was downsizing the monarchy's Advisory Council by slashing the number of advisors. But to hear that he might be passed over for the throne was shocking. There must be more to King Khalid's decision.

"Why the rush?" Imani asked.

"As you know, I went to see my father yesterday. Almost immediately, the conversation took an unexpected turn."

He told her everything they discussed, his responses, and his father's decision to pass him over.

Imani sat stunned, with a hand covering her mouth and sadness in her heart. "Wasim, I'm so sorry. King Khalid will truly be missed."

The king was tough but beloved because he was open-minded and had made decisions that impacted the country in positive ways.

Wasim nodded. "He doesn't want anyone to know yet, so please don't tell your uncle. He wants to disclose his medical condition on his own terms." Her uncle, King Babatunde, and King Khalid were friends.

"A few weeks isn't a lot of time," she said.

"No, it's not," Wasim said, his cheekbones sharpening with grief. He sighed heavily. "I'm angry that he's skipping over me, but at the same time I feel as if I've let him down. He's always mentioned his desire for me to marry, and I didn't. Now this happens. Yasmin is married with a child and another on the way, and even Akmal seems to have found someone."

"What? I didn't know Akmal was getting married," Imani said.

"I understand your shock. He can be quite irresponsible, but he's had his eye on a member of the royal family in Jordan. The families have been in talks, and now they're in the middle of negotiating the *nikah*," he said.

"If Akmal, who is younger than you is on his way to getting married, what's stopping you? And that's not a rhetorical question. Why haven't you married? Why don't you have any prospects?"

"I'm like you. I haven't found the right person yet."

She glanced out the window and then looked at him again. "What are you going to do, Wasim?"

"What can I do? I don't have time to find a wife to put my father's mind at ease. And then thinking about everything I have to do with him dying..." He swallowed down the pain. "The truth is, there is too much work to be done to worry about marriage. His administration and the family and I need to focus in the coming weeks. We don't have much time. I will do whatever I can to give my father peace of mind and work with his successor as he wishes to use me."

They both fell silent, each in their own thoughts. Imani was in a state of shock. King Khalid was dying and Wasim, his presumptive successor, would not succeed him.

Then she had an idea—wild and radical and completely outrageous, but...it might work, in both their favors.

She lowered her voice so that if anyone stood near the open door, they couldn't hear. "This is going to sound crazy, but hear me out."

"I'm listening."

She leaned toward him. "We could help each other. You want the throne and want your father to pass in peace. You can't have him worrying about the kingdom in his last days, and he admitted he thought you'd be a great ruler. I need my parents to leave me alone instead of trying to force a man on me that I don't want. A man who will probably try to keep me from accomplishing all the goals I have because I'll be tied down as his wife and mother of his children. Here is my solution: We should pretend to be engaged."

Wasim stared at her. "Pretend?"

"Yes. Think about it. I'm a noblewoman—a member of the royal family of Zamibia, one of Barrakesch's most trusted allies. I'm accomplished, I know your family, and they know me and my character." She stopped talking and waited for his response.

He frowned doubtfully. "I don't know what to say."

"Say yes."

"You're not talking about actually getting married, but pretending we want a future together?"

Imani nodded.

"And then when my father passes...?"

"We wait a while and then split up, going our separate ways, amicably. What do you think?"

6

He thought she was crazy.

Despite that, Imani's idea could work. Though Wasim hated to think about it, his father only had a few weeks to live. He'd considered putting together a list of potential wives, but the truth was, he didn't want to get married now, and with less than a week to find someone before his father's announcement, that idea had quickly been dismissed.

But this idea—pretending he and Imani were going to get married—would allow him to accomplish everything he wanted to—take the throne which was rightfully his and ease his father's concerns.

"We already know a lot about each other," Imani continued, pressing her advantage. "How many siblings do I have?"

"Six brothers," Wasim answered.

"What's my favorite color?"

"Lavender, though gold runs a close second."

"What's the one thing I want to accomplish more than anything else?"

"You want to close the deal on the oil drilling project."

"See, you know me." She grinned at him.

"And you know me." He sighed heavily and thrust his fingers through his thick hair. "I wish we didn't have to do this. I wish I had more time."

Imani stretched her fingers toward him but quickly pulled back and let her hand fall to the seat beside her.

His jaw tightened because he wanted her comforting touch, but he understood her reluctance. Though no one could see them, they adhered to the rules of the country when here. They were not married. Except to shake hands, they were not supposed to touch.

"I can't remember the last time I lied to my father," Wasim said quietly.

Imani looked at him with kind and thoughtful eyes. "Don't think of it as a lie. You deserve to be king, Wasim. There is no one else better to lead the country than you. Your father knows this, so think of what we plan to do as a way to give King Khalid the peace that he needs. "

The plan involved deception but would be best for both he and Imani, as well as his father, and allow Wasim time to concentrate on learning as much as he could before having to take control of the kingdom. He would be the one to lead his country into the next decades. He would be the one to take up the mantle of his father's projects and see them through to the end. And he would be the one to continue their lineage when he found the right wife.

There was so much for him to learn, and the expectations would begin right away—had already begun. The past two days had been filled with private meetings between Wasim, his father, and his father's closest advisors.

"Your parents would be pleased. Your potential husband would be a future king instead of a businessman."

"Certainly an upgrade, and would get them off my back for a while. When you and I break up, I'm sure they'll leave me alone so I can nurse my broken heart. There's so much I could accomplish during that period."

"What about your Senegalese suitor?" Wasim asked, the thought of her and any other man souring his stomach.

"He's not a problem now, and we could start dating and getting to know each other later."

Wasim stood and moved restlessly, rubbing the back of his neck. "So we break up, at a time of our choosing?"

"Yes. Amicably, of course."

"There is one problem that we haven't considered. You're not Muslim, and while my father and aunt probably won't have a problem with that, there are conservatives in the Parliament who would. Any chance you'd be willing to convert to Islam?"

"Any chance you'd be willing to convert to Christianity?" She arched a brow.

Wasim let out a soft laugh, the first since he'd received the bad news from his father. "We're not really getting married, so it shouldn't be a problem. But I thought you should be prepared for some backlash."

She tilted her chin higher. "I can handle it. So we're all set. You'll get your birthright, and when you're ready you'll find and marry that intelligent, *obedient* woman who's good with kids."

"And you'll be able to marry your funny, smart business-man," Wasim said, the words tasting like the remnants of burnt ashes on his tongue. "We both get what we want...eventually."

"Yes," Imani said quietly.

The air became unnaturally heavy with the softly spoken word and her eyes veered away from his. Wasim could often read women, and there were times he believed he saw interest from Imani. Were those moments his imagination or not? Had that kiss in Estoria affected her as much as it affected him? Did she think about the way he made her feel, the way he frequently relived the pleasures of her mouth and the softness of her body wedged between him and the wall?

"So, do we have a deal?" Imani asked.

"We have a deal."

"As soon as you give me the all-clear, I'll let my father know to expect a call about our pending marriage, though I don't expect any objections from him. It will be quite the upgrade, going from a businessman to a crown prince," Imani said dryly, standing.

"We're really going to do this? You're sure you want to do this?" Wasim examined her face for any sign of hesitation.

In some ways they were very much alike. He was drawn to her rebellious nature and the way she did as she pleased, running headfirst into any problem and tackling it with skill and calm.

"Positive. Are you?"

No, he wasn't positive. Something in his gut warned that their plan could present problems for them both. They had to be very careful.

"This will be good for us both. I should go now. I have a lot to think about," he said instead. He led the way out of the office and stopped at the front door. "I'll be in touch."

~

THE NEXT DAY, Wasim called to let Imani know that his aunt and father approved of their engagement, and King Khalid believed their marriage was an excellent way to strengthen the alliance between their countries.

Then Imani called her parents to let them know that the king would be calling to speak to her father. Her mother's shriek of pleasure had her pulling the phone away from her ear, and she almost felt guilty about the tangible excitement coming down the phone line.

She wasn't privy to the conversation between her father—Prince Kehinde—and King Khalid, but after they talked, both men gave their blessing, paving the way for a harmonious marriage.

Her father's swift acceptance of Wasim's offer of marriage disappointed and hurt Imani—that he was so willing to marry her off, without once checking to see how she felt about the situation. He would never marry off one of her brothers in the same manner. Just like he would never make offhand comments about her brothers' fiery tempers just because they wanted to control their own destiny. She might have been married off already if she hadn't appealed to her uncle, the king, for the ambassador post in Barrakesch as soon as she finished graduate school.

A few days later, King Khalid made a formal announcement naming Wasim as his successor to the throne and announced his engagement to Imani. The days following the announcement were spent in a flurry of activity. Imani fielded numerous phone calls from friends in Barrakesch, some teasing her for snatching up one of the most eligible bachelors in the world. No surprise there, since no matter their age, women developed heart eyes and engaged in excessive giggling in his presence. A few not-so-jokingly expressed envy that she'd snagged the crown prince and future king.

Her staff expressed their congratulations and best wishes. Several of them stated they'd suspected something was going on between her and Wasim all along. She found it interesting that people saw a relationship where there was none and believed their suspicions were now confirmed.

During that same period, she received a call from Dahlia, her cousin's wife. Dahlia was an American woman he'd married over a year ago and they now had two children—a boy and a girl. She and Imani had become close, so she wasn't surprised when Dahlia called.

"You and Wasim?" Dahlia demanded as soon as Imani answered the phone.

Imani strolled from her bedroom out onto the balcony. "I'm fine, and how are you?"

Dahlia laughed. "Excuse my abrupt greeting, but you have to admit that this is a bit of a surprise. Or is it? I suspected there was an attraction or *something* going on between the two of you a long time ago."

Why was everyone saying that? What did they see besides mild flirtation? It's not as if she and Wasim didn't have other relationships. He had his secret and not-so-secret liaisons, and she had a string of "toads" she'd had to walk away from.

"Barrakesch has religious restrictions against dating, so I assure you there was nothing going on between us." Moving forward, she and Wasim would have to be extra careful about being alone together to avoid any semblance of impropriety.

"Oh, I didn't know that. Well, there was definitely an attraction there, and I told Kofi that."

Kofi spoke next. "She seems to think I didn't notice the way you two were with each other. My only surprise is that neither my cousin nor my best friend saw fit to tell me first that they were engaged. I had to hear the news from my father."

"Thanks for making me feel guilty," Imani said with a smile, leaning a shoulder against the door jamb.

"I'm surprised by this development because you've been dating quite a bit," Kofi said.

"You make it sound like I've been going through a bunch of men! There weren't that many."

"There weren't?" Kofi asked in a mocking voice.

"And what about Wasim? No comment about the number of women you've seen him involved with?" This was the type of conversation that irritated her. The men in her family insisted on treating her differently because they didn't see her as an equal.

"It was obvious to me for a long time that Wasim was smitten with you, despite the other women."

Her heart lurched with such unexpected news. "What makes you say that?"

"I have two eyes and could see the way he looked at you."

Imani gnawed on the corner of her bottom lip. Had Wasim looked at her in some special way? Before or after that intimate moment in Estoria?

"I'm very happy for the two of you, and I'm excited for the wedding," Dahlia said, breaking into her train of thought.

"There won't be a wedding anytime soon. Wasim is preoccupied with getting everything ready for when his father passes. As morbid as that sounds, it's important for the smooth transition of power. A wedding is the last thing on either of our minds."

"I'm so sorry to hear about his father. Of course this is a difficult time, and I know that you'll provide much of the support that he needs."

"I'll certainly do my best."

"When will we see you again?" Kofi asked.

"Once I wrap up my post here, in about a month."

Dahlia spoke next. "We look forward to seeing you then, and at that time we'll have some kind of celebration."

"I'll plan on it," Imani said.

"All right, we won't keep you. Goodbye," Dahlia said.

"Goodbye. Kiss the little ones for me."

"I will. See you soon!"

After another round of goodbyes, Imani hung up the phone. She touched a finger to her bottom lip and felt warmth pool in her pelvis. Had those looks Kofi said he saw from Wasim been mere lust...or something more?

"YOU AND IMANI? I suppose I shouldn't be surprised," Andres said.

Sitting at the top of the steps that led into his expansive back yard, Wasim smiled at Andres's incredulous tone. He scratched under the chin of the baby lion wedged up against his thigh. She was absolutely adorable, purring happily with half-closed eyes as he scratched her pleasure spot.

Across the lawn, the animal caretakers playfully wrestled with the lion and lioness in the grass.

"There was always chemistry between the two of you, but I never thought anything would come of it," Andres admitted.

That comment got Wasim's attention. "And why not?"

"For one thing, I never saw any sign of you settling down."

"That's because I didn't want to settle down. But circumstances change, and decisions have to be made that make sense for you and your future."

"That sounds very romantic," Andres said dryly.

"What did you hope for? That she would put a ring through my nose the way Angela has put a ring through yours?"

A mere four months ago, in December, he'd married Angela Lipscomb, Dahlia's best friend. He met her at Dahlia and Kofi's wedding. They had a baby on the way in a few months.

Andres laughed. "Yes, and that you would love every minute of it. Falling in love and being with the person you love is the best feeling in the world. It makes you willing to do anything to hold on to that high."

Wasim rubbed his hand over the cub's head and ears, but didn't reply.

"You don't have to answer me, but I have to ask—is this real?"

Wasim paused. "What do you mean?"

"You and Imani."

"As real as ever," he replied evenly.

"That's not an answer."

"You have doubts because...why, exactly?"

"The timing, I suppose. But maybe I'm wrong."

Wasim's gaze shifted to where the adult lions now lazed in the sun. "Imani has all the qualities I want in a wife."

"And she understands the demands that come with that position, which makes her a good fit. I'm happy for you, if this is what you want."

"This is what I want," Wasim said firmly.

"Then I wish you both the best."

"Thank you." He had a feeling they would need it.

7

What a day!

Imani hurried into the embassy and removed her white face mask. She felt grimy and dirty. Today had been a particularly scorching day, with the ceremony she attended getting cut short by a sandstorm. They hadn't had one this bad in over a year. With limited visibility, the entire city looked like it was covered in fog, and the local weather service predicted those conditions would remain until tomorrow.

Thank goodness she'd worn another headscarf, turban-style again—gold and black this time—which matched her gold blouse and black slacks. She looked forward to a cleansing shower, but at least she wouldn't have to wash her hair.

"Any messages?" she asked as she swept down the carpeted hall to her office, past the photographs that portrayed rural and city life in Zamibia. She tucked the mask into the large leather purse over her shoulder.

Daman, the office manager, fell into step beside her and brushed dust particles from her clothes. He was a few inches taller than her with dark brown skin and wore his hair in dreadlocks pinned in a bun at the crown of his head.

"A few phone calls inquiring about the result of the report from the environmental commission."

"A report we still haven't received yet," Imani said, irritation spiking her voice.

"Nothing has changed since this morning, and I've called several times to get an update, but no one can tell me anything except they will provide the report soon."

Waiting for the assessment put Imani and her team in an awkward position with the Barrakesch government. Once the report arrived, they'd have to sort through it and make final adjustments before the agreement between Barrakesch and Zamibia could be signed. But absolutely nothing could be done until then. Right now, the Barrakesch Ministry of Oil was patient, but the delay meant postponing getting this project off all their plates.

"Keep me up to date on—"

Imani came to a stop on the threshold of her office and stared at her favorite piece of furniture. The large, heavy desk had been imported from Zamibia at her request and right now served as the base for a vase filled with red roses. She walked forward slowly.

"What's all this?" She lifted one of the roses from the enormous bouquet.

"Special delivery. They arrived after lunch." Daman came to stand beside her.

"From who?" Imani opened the attached envelope. Only one short sentence was written on the card inside.

No more toads.

Her heart fluttered, and she smiled through the biting of her lip.

Damon leaned in and peered at the card. "No more toads?"

Imani clutched the message to her chest and pursed her lips. "Mind your business."

"What does that mean?"

Instead of answering, Imani walked around the desk, set down her purse, and sat in the leather chair. Crossing her legs, she sniffed the petals of the single rose, which reminded her of how the front entrance of Wasim's home smelled. Roses were among the flowers he used in the fountain in the foyer.

"Don't you have work to do?" she asked pointedly.

"So you're not going to tell me?"

"*Bye*, Daman."

"Those better be from Prince Wasim, or I'm telling." He sent her a pointed look as he walked out of the room.

Imani failed at fighting the smile that came to her face. Wasim certainly had his own cheerleading section. She didn't doubt for a minute that Daman would rat her out to Wasim if she stepped out of line. Women loved him and men admired him.

Her gaze lingered on the beautiful flowers, and she tapped a finger on the desktop. Should she call him now? He might be busy, but she wanted to thank him.

"Call him now," she said aloud, laughing to herself.

She dialed his number, and it rang three times before he answered.

"Hello, Prince Wasim." Imani winced, embarrassed at the sound of her voice. She sounded extra sweet and downright coquettish.

"Hello, Ambassador Karunzika. Did you get my gift? I hope the color was okay. I couldn't find lavender roses."

When he talked like that, with his voice low and warmth seeping through the words, he made her pulse go crazy.

"Yes, I received them and the color is fine. The flowers are beautiful. Toads?" She smiled.

"I'm wishing you the best moving forward. You're too good for the toads of the world."

Her nipples tightened fractionally. The compliment and small gesture of sending flowers had her head floating above the clouds.

This is pretend, she reminded herself.

"Thank you. That was very thoughtful. How are things coming with the technology expo?"

"Looking good so far. I expect it to be very successful."

"Not bad for your first time."

"Not bad at all," he agreed.

"How is he?" Imani asked gently. She'd gone to spend time with the king the other day, and it was never clearer that death was nigh.

"Doing well, though it seems since he knows the kingdom will be fine, the weight that has been taken off his shoulders has made him more relaxed. Almost as if he's...letting go." His voice thickened toward the end.

Imani shut her eyes and absorbed his pain. "If there's anything I can do, you'll let me know, won't you? I hope you know I mean that."

"I will. And Imani, thank you for doing this."

"Of course. We're helping each other, right?"

"Right."

Pause.

"In a few days I'm playing host to some men from the United States who want to open businesses here. We invited them to come with their families to my home. As my fiancée, I think it would be a good idea for you to attend. I'd considered canceling the event, but my father insisted I should move forward with the plans. Farouk and Yasmin will be there."

"I know how you Barrakeschis love any reason to get together and eat. Is this one of your weed-them-out events?"

Family bonds were an important part of the culture. So

important that large families were encouraged, and relatives often lived together in the same neighborhoods, creating community clusters that shared child-rearing duties and elder-care. Whenever possible, Wasim preferred to do business with people who held the same family values and liked to invite potential business partners to his home to see how they interacted with their spouses and children in a social setting.

He chuckled. "Yes."

"That's so unfair—these men have no idea you're judging them."

"It wouldn't be an effective test if they did. So, I'll see you in a few days? It will be more enjoyable if you're there."

Imani's cheeks heated at the compliment. Because of their friendship she'd attended royal family functions in the past, but she'd never been to one of these type of events. "I'll see you in a few days, Wasim."

After they hung up, Imani sat staring at the bouquet. Then she lifted the single rose to her nose and inhaled its fragrance.

8

W asim shook hands with the first American businessman who arrived with his nine-year-old daughter and wife by his side.

"Quite the spread you have here, Prince Wasim," the man said, looking around.

"Thank you. Please, make yourself at home. There is plenty to eat and drink, and we even have a little entertainment for you." He pointed in the direction of the animals that had been placed behind a wire fence to separate them from the guests.

The little girl squealed. "Is that a lion?"

"It is. I have two and a cub, two tigers, and chimpanzees," Wasim answered.

"Oooh, Dad, can I go see?" She bounced on her feet.

The American chuckled. "Go right ahead, but be careful." As she tore off across the lawn, he turned to Wasim. "Interesting pets."

"They make great conversation starters," Wasim said with a chuckle. "Excuse me while I check on the other guests."

As Imani had pointed out, Barrakeschis loved a good party and loved to eat, so parties and plenty of good food always went hand in hand. Caterers had set up tables around the lawn filled with an eclectic menu that was typically Middle Eastern but also included choices from the Indians and other Asians whose food had influenced the country since making it their home.

Wasim strolled across the lawn in a white long-sleeved shirt and black slacks, pleased with the turnout, but wondering where Imani could be. Being that they were now officially a couple, they had to avoid the appearance of impropriety and be even more careful than usual about being seen alone together, so today's group event was an opportunity for them to spend time together while maintaining the ruse that they planned to marry.

Once again, the thought of his father's passing hit him. He was glad to be able to continue his father's work and the plans he himself had envisioned, but it was nonetheless sobering to know that he would lose his father soon, essentially any day now.

Farouk and Yasmin arrived, holding hands like newlyweds, with Malak skipping along ahead of them. After a quick greeting, his nephew immediately ran off to play with the other children, tossing a ball on the grass.

Wasim crisscrossed the lawn, mingling with the guests and stopping to tease the children. As he greeted a small group of adults playing horseshoes, his sentence trailed off when Imani exited the house and stood at the top of the steps.

For a moment, he was speechless. He'd never seen her hair like that before, parted on one side and flipped up at the ends. She wore a mustard-colored tunic and matching pants. Brownish-red lipstick complemented her bronze complexion and coated the fullness of her lips, drawing his eyes and hurtling him back in time to the taste of that same mouth and how much he'd enjoyed kissing her.

He quickly abandoned the guests and walked over to her. Smiling, she stepped down onto the grass.

"Hi."

"You finally decided to make an appearance. How nice of you to show up...late."

"You didn't give me a specific time, and you should be glad I'm here considering you begged me to come."

"Let's not exaggerate. I invited you."

"Because this wouldn't be much of a party without me. You're welcome."

"I didn't thank you."

"You were about to."

Wasim laughed. He'd miss their verbal sparring when she went back to Zamibia.

"I see you're doing something different with your hair." He hadn't planned to comment on her hairstyle, but the words just came out of him.

Imani fingered the strands, suddenly more subdued. "I'm trying something different."

"I like it."

She glanced at him. "Thank you."

"You're wearing a different scent, too."

Her eyebrows raised a little in surprise.

She had no idea the close attention he paid to everything about her—her clothes, hair, the scents she wore.

"I am wearing a different scent. Normally it's shea butter infused with passionfruit, but I'm trying a new fragrance from a line of creams and lotions made locally by the women's cooperative of Zamibia. This one is shea butter infused with mango."

She was truly amazing. Imani didn't only publicize and encourage the women's work, she supported them by buying their products. She'd also worked out a way to invest in their businesses with money from the oil revenues once they started pouring in.

"I like it," Wasim said. She smelled so good he wished he could carry the scent of her with him at all times.

"You're full of compliments today."

"You deserve every one."

Before she could reply, Malak ran over, squealing excitedly at the sight of Imani. Dropping to her haunches, she gave him a big hug and kissed both of his cheeks. "Oh my goodness, look at you! You're getting so big. How old are you now?"

"Four." He held up four fingers.

Her eyes widened. "I better be careful or you'll catch up to me soon."

Malak's little face brightened from laughter. "Do you want to see my chimpanzees?" he asked.

"Wait a minute, they're your chimpanzees now?" Wasim asked.

"Yes." The little boy giggled.

Wasim folded his arms across his chest and affected a stern expression. "You bought them?"

His nephew nodded vigorously.

"Where did you get money?"

"When I went to the hotel to work with *Baba*," he replied.

"Now you know," Imani said with a laugh as she let Malak pull her away.

Wasim kept his eyes on her regal walk. Rubbing his bearded cheek, he let his gaze swing back and forth with the movement of her hips. She could make any outfit sexy—including a loose-fitting tunic and pants that did more to hide her figure than display it.

Her legs were completely covered, yet he couldn't help but notice how she moved with effortless sensuality. Perhaps because he knew what lay under the clothes. Outside of Barrakesch, he'd seen her toned legs in fitted skirts that showed off her curvaceous shape and plump bottom. He'd had many thoughts about getting his hands on that ass.

Imani sat down on a rug on the lawn and proceeded to play with Malak and five other kids. They fed bananas to the chimp and cuddled with the lion cub, who practiced its roar—which sounded more like a squeak.

"You made a good choice." Yasmin had sidled up beside him.

"You think so?" Wasim shifted his gaze to look at his sister. At four months pregnant, she only had the smallest baby bump.

Yasmin nodded. "You're the perfect match. I don't think you could have done better. We all like her." She sauntered over to a bench where Farouk sat and joined him.

Wasim went back to mingling with the guests but remained attuned to Imani's every movement. His sister's words resonated with him.

Imani was perfect. Where would he find another woman who fit so perfectly within his culture and life? An equal. A woman whose deep love for her country made her put in long hours on the oil drilling project because it would improve the country's economy. There was no better woman to have by his side as a life partner.

But their entire relationship was fake. Made up. Not real.

But what if it wasn't?

"Okay, cuties. I need to take a break."

"Aww," the group of kids moaned as Imani stood. They were great for her ego.

"Five minutes and then I'll be back."

She made her way over to the refreshments table and poured herself a citrus water. Quite a few people milled around the lawn, but her attention went immediately to Wasim and a member of his staff chatting near the fenced-in lions and tigers.

One hour and thirty minutes.

That's how long she'd been there, while at the same time

wondering why she'd come. She'd almost changed her mind about showing up because she wasn't exactly sure what was happening to her.

She'd changed her hairstyle to grab his attention because... because he sent her flowers. How silly, but that's exactly what happened. The fact that he noticed her hair and liked the style made her happy, and so she couldn't get the darn flowers off her mind.

They meant nothing because she and he were simply two friends helping each other, yet the roses sat on a table in her bedroom, basking in the sunlight that came in through the window. Proving, in effect, that they were not nothing by their prominent position in the room.

"Hello, Ambassador." A blond-haired man gave her a friendly smile.

"Hello." She didn't recognize him, though after he'd arrived she noticed him wandering from person to person striking up conversations. Each time, after a few minutes, the people sauntered away and left him alone.

"Mark Strouse, with RollTech Industries out of Seattle."

He extended a hand and she took it.

"It's nice to meet you."

He clasped his other hand over hers and leaned in. "I have to tell you, I just spoke to someone who has nothing but good things to say about you."

"Oh?"

Now she knew why people were leaving him alone. He smelled like liquor. It was illegal to publicly consume alcohol in Barrakesch, so those who drank did so at home. Clearly Mark had done some pre-party drinking—probably at a hotel, in his case. And he'd had no qualms doing so in the middle of the afternoon.

"Yes, indeed. I'm impressed by your women empowerment

projects and the fact that you're the youngest ambassador ever to be assigned to Barrakesch."

Imani tried to ease her hand from his grasp. "Well, someone has to do it."

Mark let go with one hand, but tightened the other. At this point, he'd held onto her too long.

He looked into her eyes. "Forgive me for being forward, but you're an incredibly beautiful woman. I thought you should know that." He finally dropped her hand, but then stepped close and placed it on the small of her back. "Can I get you something to drink?"

Imani stiffened. Living in Barrakesch, she'd become accustomed to men keeping a respectful distance and being more mannerly in their interactions with the opposite sex. Mark made her uneasy.

She stepped away from his touch. "No, I'm fine. You know, I'm going over here with the kids—"

"Excuse me. I don't believe we've met." Wasim came up beside them. "Mark Strouse, isn't that correct?" He stuck out his hand.

"Prince Wasim! No, we haven't." Mark shook his hand vigorously.

"Welcome. I didn't get a chance to speak to you earlier. I hope you've been enjoying yourself."

"I have. As a matter of fact, Ambassador Karunzika has been the best part of the day so far." His gaze flicked over her in an inappropriate way.

"Better than meeting me?" Wasim asked.

"Afraid so. Nothing takes the place of a beautiful woman."

Imani gave him a tight smile.

Wasim's astute gaze bounced between the two of them. "How is your wife?" he asked.

Mark gave him a startled glance. "Er, fine. She couldn't make the trip."

"I'm sure it's difficult to fly when you're seven months pregnant."

"Yes, yes it is," Mark said slowly, obviously surprised by how much Wasim knew about him.

"You realize now that you've made a mistake, don't you?" Wasim asked. "You should have done what you Americans like to say—read the room. There are a few things you must learn. First, you do not touch a woman in the manner you just did. It is inappropriate."

"I'm sorry, I didn't know," Mark said.

"You also clearly didn't know that Ambassador Karunzika is my fiancée."

Mark's eyes widened and an *oh-shit* expression came on his face. "Your fiancée?"

"That's correct. In light of your behavior, I'm going to have to ask you to leave. We won't be doing business together."

"I just got here." Mark laughed uncomfortably, glancing at Imani as if she could rescue him. "I made a mistake. I didn't mean—"

"I'll have someone show you the way out." Wasim waved over one of the attendants, who started toward them.

Mark straightened and cleared his throat. "This isn't how I expected the day to progress, but thank you for the opportunity. I hope you'll change your mind about us doing business in the future."

Not likely, Imani thought, if the impassive expression on Wasim's face was anything to go by.

After Mark was escorted away, Wasim said, "He smells as if he's spent the better part of the day drinking. You should have gotten my attention when he started bothering you."

"I could handle him."

"You shouldn't have to," he grated. He spoke quietly so as not draw attention.

"Are you scolding me?" Imani asked in an equally low voice.

"Yes, because you should have called me over."

Imani said in a low voice, "We're not really in a relationship, so I—"

"Everyone thinks we are," Wasim interrupted. His copper-brown eyes flashed with ill-disguised anger. "And he had no right to touch you—or any other woman here, for that matter —like that. He wasn't aware of our cultural norms, nor that you and I are a couple—real or not. He missed a lot, wouldn't you say? He couldn't be bothered to learn a little bit about the country he's visiting or the man he's trying to do business with, and dared to make a pass at you. Next time, let me know."

"You're right. I...I'm used to taking care of myself, that's all." Imani shrugged.

"If you were mine, you'd never have to," Wasim rasped. Then he stalked away toward a group of guests.

Imani stared after him.

What in the world did he mean by that?

9

W asim sat on the back steps of his palace, eyes focused on the lights of Kabatra in the distance. All the guests had gone home and the servants had cleared away any evidence of the party.

He'd decided to do business with two of the men who'd come today. Their knowledge, values, and behavior had impressed him.

A shadow fell across the steps.

"Will there be anything else, Your Highness?" The question came from a servant behind him.

"No. Have a good night."

"Good night, Your Highness."

His pet chimpanzee sauntered over and rested her head on his knee, as if to keep him company or lift his spirits. Wasim absentmindedly petted her head, his thoughts going elsewhere —to the night in Estoria when he kissed Imani. They'd been in the country for a polo tournament and ended up alone in his hotel room. Since then their friendship had remained intact, uneventful except for the deeper undercurrent of attraction between them.

They wouldn't work. They both knew that. Neither of them was ready for marriage, and besides, their ideas about marriage were different.

Yet he couldn't stop thinking about that night.

TEN MONTHS *ago*

"So you've never tasted alcohol, not even once?"

Wasim looked across the table at Imani, with her liquid brown eyes that had called to him all day. She seemed much more relaxed than earlier when she'd first arrived at his door, agitated and trying to find her cousin, Kofi, after a conversation with her parents. She'd been disappointed to learn that he had gone out for drinks with some of the men who had participated in the polo match earlier. Wasim had stayed behind, preferring to relax in the room and get a little work done before going to bed.

Since he was about to order dinner, he invited her in and listened to her complaints about her father and his dismissive tone regarding her desires for her love life. She simply wanted to be left alone to live her own life and make her own decisions, but that seemed to be an impossibility for her parents—especially her father. He saw her as a little girl who needed to be protected and wanted to see her married and taken care of, despite her many accomplishments over the years.

"I've never once tasted alcohol," Wasim confirmed, taking a sip of iced tea.

The meal had been finished an hour ago, but they sat there talking, spending more time alone than he could ever remember in the past. He and Imani knew each other well, but this particular conversation felt more personal, more intimate. Maybe it was the hotel room. Or maybe it was the fact that they had never been alone for such a long period. For three hours they had sat in his suite in the Royal Palace of Estoria and simply enjoyed each other's company. Laughing, talking, and sharing intimate details like old friends.

"I had no idea. You've never been curious?"

"Curious, but not enough to try." He shrugged. "Drinking alcohol is *haram* in Islam."

She cocked her head to the side, studying him for a moment. "Premarital sex is forbidden, as well, isn't it?"

"It is."

She smirked a little bit. "But you've had sex."

He smiled slightly. "I have rules that I live by, but I'm not perfect."

"Shocker. Your secret is safe with me."

"I appreciate that. So, what are you going to do about your parents?"

She let out a dramatic moan and let her head fall back. His eyes traveled over the length of her throat—a throat that begged to be licked and sucked. He swiped a hand over his mouth, thinking for the umpteenth time what a mistake he had made inviting her in for dinner. His body had been on red alert the entire time, more so than usual. He had always been attracted to Imani, but that attraction had become particularly acute tonight.

"I'll do what I always do. Put them off. Delay. Remind them that I can make my own decisions about my future husband."

"It's unfortunate you have to deal with that."

"You have to deal with it to a certain degree, too, don't you?"

"I have less pressure than you."

"Has your aunt given up?"

"I believe so. I hope so." He held up crossed fingers, and she giggled.

Imani yawned and set her glass of wine on the table. "I should go. It's late."

"You should." Wasim looked across the table at her, his gaze steady and unflinching. "Or you could stay."

She didn't respond, but she looked at him, and he saw movement in her throat as she swallowed.

"I don't know what you mean. I don't know where this conversation is going."

"I believe you know exactly where this conversation is going. You're not naïve, Imani. There has been something between us, almost since the first day we met. Unacknowledged during all this time, but sitting here with you and talking makes it hard to ignore."

Nervously, she licked her lips, but neither of their gazes wavered. "What you're suggesting is outside the parameters of our friendship. If this is some kind of joke..."

"Do I look like I'm joking?" When she didn't reply, he continued. "All night I've thought about kissing you, and it's not the first time."

"You can't talk to me like that." Her voice shook.

"Why not?"

"Because you can't. Because we're friends, and...friends don't talk like that."

"Then maybe we should end our friendship, because every time I'm near you, my thoughts are not friendly at all." He didn't know what possessed him to be so up-front, except the stress of his attraction to her had started to wear on him. Spending this time together created an opportunity for him to be frank and test the waters. So far she hadn't run out of the room, so he considered that a good thing.

"I should go." Imani scraped back her chair and stood.

"I didn't mean to chase you off." Wasim stood, too.

"You didn't. I'm just not sure this is the right conversation for us to be having."

"Why not?"

"Because it makes me uncomfortable, all right? I-I...it makes me uneasy."

"Why?" He walked closer. "We know each other."

"Yes, we know each other. But I also know you're not interested in a serious relationship."

"Yet. And neither are you. Your parents want you to move toward marriage, and you've been fighting it tooth and nail. We are exactly alike, you and I."

He reached up and touched her soft hair, smoothing strands back from her face. Her eyes shuttered closed, and that encouraged him to move closer—so close he smelled the sweetness of the grapes on her breath.

"Wasim..."

"I've ached to kiss you all night." He brushed his thumb across her full bottom lip. "One kiss, and I'll let you go." At least he'd try to let her go.

She gazed up at him, and her heavy breathing mingled with his slower breaths. "It won't be one kiss," she said, calling him out for the liar he was.

"Just a taste, Imani. To put me out of my misery." As the night wore on, he'd become consumed with one objective—to satisfy a need for her that had long been denied.

Their eyes locked for a moment, and then he lowered his lips to hers.

When their mouths met, the breath stalled in his lungs and his body stiffened under the weight of shock and awareness. He'd known the kiss would be pleasurable, but that small sample was already *exquisite*. Unexpected bliss swept away every sound and scent in the vicinity and had his senses focused on the sensation of her soft body pressed against his and the sweetness of her filling his nostrils.

He found himself cupping her face with his other hand and sucking on her bottom lip, for the first time tasting wine as he dipped his tongue along the inside of her mouth. But the flavor paled in comparison to the taste of Imani.

She whimpered, pressing her pelvis against his and clutching at his upper arms. Her moaning and the way she gripped his biceps made him feel invincible, powerful. As if he was strong enough to clear mountains out of her path.

She stepped backward and he followed, pressing her into the wall. With a low growl, his tongue penetrated her lips and licked at the moisture within, and he thrust long fingers into her short, silky hair as he grasped the back of her neck. He held her firm, keeping her in place so he could have more.

He urged her lips wider as he assaulted her with his tongue and swallowed her gasp. Her own fingers lifted into his hair, and a shudder rocked his frame as her short nails scraped at his scalp.

Wasim could feel himself losing control, practically bursting at the seams for the opportunity to sink into her, finally, after lusting after her for years. Partially out of respect for his good friend, Kofi, he'd kept his distance. But with her tight little body pressed up against his, heat licking at his skin wherever her roaming hands wandered, the battle of resistance would be lost tonight because his erection stood heavy like a cylinder of lead between his thighs. If he didn't get a chance to have this woman he might explode.

Wasim lifted Imani against the wall and pressed the full weight of his erection between her thighs. She groaned as he did a teasing grind, showing her what she was missing, what he could offer if she only let him in.

"One night." He licked her neck and his teeth nipped at her sensitive skin. "I promise that I..." He couldn't finish the sentence. His voice, hoarse and hungry, didn't sound at all princely. He sounded desperate and was shameless in his need for her.

He lowered her to the floor and slipped both hands under her dress. He grasped both sides of her panties and was about to yank them down to her ankles when she grabbed his wrists.

"Wait. Stop." She was panting, but he clearly heard the words.

Wasim rested his forehead on the wall right above her shoulder. "Imani..." he said in a gravelly voice.

"I can't." She whispered the words against the beating pulse of his throat.

Wasim closed his eyes. "Why?" The ache in his loins was going to eat him alive.

She pushed against his chest to create distance between them and with deep reluctance, he stepped back.

He watched her in the momentary silence. Downcast eyes. Heaving breaths. He'd kissed off her lipstick and exposed the raw beauty of her succulent lips, now swollen to more provocative fullness.

"A couple of years ago, I promised myself that the next man I have sex with will be my husband. I guess we both have rules that we live by." She lifted her eyes to his. "We should pretend this never happened and stick to friendship, don't you agree?"

Years? Imani hadn't been made love to in *years*?

Wasim didn't reply to her question. He would have to respect her wishes, but he didn't agree. Because his loins burned with desire for her, the flames flaring hotter now that he knew about her abstinence. If she said one little three-letter word—yes—he'd have her naked and on her back in seconds.

"Good night," Imani said.

Then she quietly left the room.

10

The reception in the Grand Hall of the Ritz-Carlton to kick off the first Kabatra Technology Expo was filled with the biggest names in the tech world, with representatives from countries on six of the world's continents. Tonight, Imani wore a simple black pants suit and wrapped her hair turban-style in a black and red Ankara-print scarf, accentuating the look with gold hoops in her ears and bold red lipstick.

She hoped to make contacts tonight that would facilitate future business deals to benefit the tech companies in Zamibia. In addition, she had invited two of the biggest names in Zamibian cybersecurity and had spent the better part of the afternoon prepping them for tonight. Both—one a woman and the other a man—seemed to be doing well so far, but she kept a close eye on them nonetheless.

For now, though, as she walked the room shaking hands and making conversation, her mind remained preoccupied with thoughts of Wasim. After Sunday, the memory of their kiss in Estoria came back with a vengeance and reminded her of what it was like to have his hands and mouth on her. She couldn't believe she'd managed to resist him. *One night,* he'd whispered, and she'd been sorely tempted to give in. Thank goodness he hadn't pushed harder.

"Hello, Ambassador," one of the attendees said. They shook hands and chatted for a few minutes. Then Imani got a ginger ale and went to stand on the edge of the room.

Wasim's assertiveness with Mark had been...appealing, and the thought of being taken care of lingered like the after-taste of a sweet pastry. One she definitely wanted more bites of.

She shook her head in disgust. She was losing it. The man had actually used the word *mine*. His ideas were archaic. She was Lioness Abameha Imani Karunzika, Zamibian Ambas-sador to Barrakesch. The thought of *belonging* to a man was nauseating. She was independent and knew her own mind.

She would never *belong* to a man, but if she did, it certainly wouldn't be Prince Wasim of Barrakesch. She'd grown up around men like him who were used to having power and their authority unquestioned. She couldn't thrive in a relationship like that. She'd suffocate under the limitations he was sure to impose.

A spattering of applause filled the air, and Imani turned to see that Wasim had finally arrived. He looked handsome in a dark three-piece suit with a pale pink tie. He wore his hair brushed back from his face and had tamed it into a semblance of order, though one lone curl managed to go rogue and fall to right above his left eyebrow. When he flashed a smile, lifting his hand in greeting to the attendees, she let loose a slow breath to calm her racing heart.

He found her in the crowd, and when their eyes met, she tipped her glass of ginger ale to him, and a minute smile lifted the corner of his mouth. Not a full smile, though—as if he wasn't completely in the best of spirits. The vibrancy in his eyes was missing, and there was an emptiness there she wasn't used to seeing. Then the crowd converged, and his attention was taken up by the people who surrounded him.

The night continued in the same vein it had started— conversations with potential partners, exchanging business cards, snacking and drinking, and more talking. After her two invitees left, Imani took a seat at a corner bistro table and watched the thinning crowd.

She checked her watch. She'd stick around for another half hour or so and then leave so she could get up early in the morning for the first day of the expo. She was scheduled to do a speech at the opening breakfast and wanted to get home in time to practice one more time and get plenty of rest for the event.

Wasim approached, stopping briefly to speak to two men from Saudi Arabia before finally making his way over to her. He set down his glass of water and stood beside the table, resting an arm on the flat surface. His cologne, with the under-lying scent of oud, filled the space between them.

"Hiding?" The inviting sound of his dark, sinful voice washed over her.

"Taking a short break until I have to make my rounds before I leave for the night."

Wasim nodded. He remained quiet for a while, then, "I owe you an apology for my behavior the other day, at the party at my house. I acted like an ass."

"*You* acted like an ass? Unheard of."

"Sarcasm is not a good look on you," Wasim said dryly.

Imani bit her bottom lip, chuckling softly.

"I have no doubt you can take care of yourself. As for Mark, I'm not sorry I kicked him out. He had no business being there and not in that state."

Imani nodded her agreement.

"What do you think about tonight? Not a bad turnout, considering this is the first time."

He'd wanted to put on this event for a while and had been working on it for several years, so she knew he was glad that it had finally come to fruition. This was one of the many ways he hoped to move the country forward, and she envisioned him being able to do much more once he became king.

"I'm impressed. If tonight is anything to go by, you can safely make this an annual event."

He nodded. "Agreed. I think it would be good to allocate slots for smaller firms the next time."

"Maybe even offer some type of funding in the form of a scholarship for small businesses who might not be able to afford to come. It would also be nice to see more women-run companies in attendance in the future, too."

He nodded thoughtfully. "I was thinking the same thing. We could set aside a couple of scholarships specifically for those reasons. When I give my father a full report, I'll mention that idea."

This was Wasim's personal project, but it was not unusual for the king to show his support by showing up to events, even if only for fifteen minutes or so. But since the announcement, he'd eliminated all public appearances.

"How has he been?"

"Not good," Wasim answered, eyes bleak.

Before she could ask him anymore questions, an Australian businessman approached. Medium-height with flaxen hair and matching eyebrows, he was a slight-looking man with dark eyes, dressed casually in chinos and a polo shirt. Imani had talked to him earlier, and he acknowledged her with a smile, but extended a hand to Wasim.

"Prince Wasim, I was wondering if I could have a moment with you," the man said with a nasal twang. "I want to talk to you about working with the royal family on a top-secret project, one that I think you'd be very interested in. I strongly believe a relationship between us could be mutually beneficial, but your chief of technology doesn't think so. At least, he's hesitant."

"Tonight is for networking, not making final deals," Wasim said, softening the chastisement with a smile. "If he seems hesitant, it's because he doesn't know you well yet."

"Understood. I suppose a better question would be, how can my company get to the head of the line, so to speak?"

"What is the name of your company?"

The Australian gave an embarrassed laugh. "I'm sorry. Heath Palmer, of P & T Technologies. I'm in business with my brother-in-law. I'd love to tell you more about my idea and how we use tracking devices in security for the rich and famous around the world." He extended a card.

Wasim turned over the card in his hand. "Have you sold many of these products?"

"Well…" Heath hedged, laughing again. "Right now we're in the beta stage and offering the technology free of charge to a limited number of clients."

"In exchange for free publicity through word-of-mouth," Wasim deduced.

"Yes," Heath admitted. "But I strongly believe you will love these. They can be placed in a piece of jewelry, the heel of a shoe, or sewn into the seam of a bag." He seemed to hold his breath as he waited for Wasim's response.

"Let's go over here for a few minutes to chat." Wasim turned to Imani. "When are you leaving?"

"In another thirty minutes or so."

"Don't leave before we get a chance to talk again."

"Pardon my rudeness. Congratulations on your engagement," Heath said, looking between them.

"Thank you," they both replied, as Imani's heart twisted a little painfully on the inside.

Wasim gave her another wry smile before leaving with the Australian.

Imani stared after him. Then she glanced at the glass of water he left behind. There was the faintest imprint of his lips at the rim, and she quickly looked away, embarrassed at the direction of her thoughts.

She shouldn't have kissed him that night, because almost every day since then she'd had some variation on that thought —*I shouldn't have kissed him.* Her cheeks heated as she quietly admitted that she wanted to place her mouth in that exact spot where he'd placed his. For a little taste, no matter how minor.

Imani abruptly stood and abandoned the table, going back to mingle among the crowd. Time was counting down, not only on King Khalid's life, but on her stay in Barrakesch. Her stomach turned in distress. The whole ruse was a bad idea and she wished she'd never suggested it.

The relationship may not be real, but these feelings she had for Wasim—these feelings were definitely real. True enough, she'd miss this country—the food, the people, the culture—her home for the past six years.

But deep down she knew she would miss Wasim most of all.

WASIM LISTENED ABSENTMINDEDLY to the owner of a Brazilian tech firm who'd been talking to him for the past five minutes. He hadn't had a chance to talk to Imani again since they spoke earlier, and he longed to break away from this conversation and spend a few minutes with her so he could decompress.

He finally located her in the room, talking to one of the few women attendees. Looking regal. Talking passionately about some topic as the woman nodded constantly. He shouldn't be surprised that she'd picked a woman to engage in conversation. By the end of the night, Imani would probably have a plan whereby the woman could compete on equal footing with the men while doubling her revenue.

The smile that had taken over his face slowly died when Wasim saw one of his father's messengers approach. With a sickening lurch, he guessed why the man had come. As he told Imani, his father had not been doing well, and he knew this was more bad news.

The man dipped his head in respect to Wasim. "Your Royal Highness, your father has requested your presence at The Grand White Palace. He is not well."

All along he'd known that at some point in the near future he would no longer have his father, and that sobering thought remained at the back of his mind as he worked tirelessly day and night and spent time with his father to learn as much as he could. It was a bittersweet time, one that he both appreciated and dreaded.

"Excuse me, I have to go," he said to the Brazilian, and took off toward Imani.

As he approached, perhaps sensing he was on his way to her, she looked in his direction. Everything he felt must have been in his face, because she excused herself from the conversation and came toward him.

Her beautiful brown eyes that normally contained a teasing light were darkened with worry. "It's King Khalid?"

Wasim nodded, his heart heavy and fear blocking his throat. She lifted her hands toward him and then clasped them together. He wanted to touch her, too. To pull her into his arms and seek the comfort he craved.

"I'll say a prayer for him, for all of you tonight," she said.

"Thank you."

With a curt nod, Wasim hurried from the room with his bodyguards. The few remaining attendees stared after them as they rushed past, but all he could think about was getting to his father's side.

11

He'd prayed often during the past two days.

Wearing a white *dishdasha* and white *taqiyah* on his head, Wasim lowered to his knees in the dimly lit prayer room and touched his forehead to the prayer mat. He remained still, only his lips moving as he uttered more prayers.

The doctors were with his father now, who earlier this evening had taken a turn for the worst since the night of the expo reception. No one was surprised, as he'd done little more than drink water the past couple of days. He'd lost his appetite and spent most of his time half-reclined out on the balcony where he could look out at the sea.

Wasim had lost his appetite, too, and worry remained an unwelcome burden in his stomach, but he did his best to hide his fears and appear strong for his father's sake. He, his siblings, and King Khalid's wives spent more time with his father the past couple of days—talking and laughing, reminiscing about holidays, birthday celebrations, and other events in the past. They reviewed old photos to refresh their memories and pretended that these happy moments could delay the inevitable.

His prayers completed, Wasim lifted from the floor and exited the prayer room. One of his father's aides stood outside.

"It's time, Prince Wasim," he said, his voice filled with the pain they all carried.

Wasim walked briskly with him through the palace to his father's bedroom. King Khalid lay prone on the bed, eyes closed, face pale. Two of his closest aides, three doctors, and Wasim's brothers surrounded him. The youngest son—a teenager—had tears running down his face, while Akmal and the other three remained stoic with somber faces.

When Wasim arrived, everyone stepped back to give him privacy with his father. The oldest son, the heir had arrived.

Wasim lowered to his knees beside the bed and held his father's hand. He closed his eyes, temporarily shielding himself from the truth—a truth he didn't want to accept, though death was part of a greater plan. Losing his father reminded him of losing his mother as a child. Now this fresh anguish would become a part of him for the unforeseen future.

King Khalid turned his head toward Wasim. His eyes opened to mere slits. "Wasim," he said in a gravelly voice.

"I'm here, *Baba*," he whispered.

He hadn't called his father that since he was child. But that's how he felt, like a child. Helpless and powerless to fight off death's tentacles as they ensnared his last living parent. Untold wealth existed at his fingertips, but he couldn't save his father.

"You must marry Imani...soon," King Khalid whispered.

At first, Wasim wasn't sure he'd understood. He sorted the words in his mind, and when he did, the sword of guilt dragged its sharp edge through his chest. He gave his father's hand a gentle squeeze.

"Promise me," King Khalid said, sounding as if he were already taking his last breath.

"Don't worry about that now. This world is no longer your concern."

"Promise me, Wasim." The words came out stronger but by his wheezing breaths, it was clear they had taken a lot of energy.

Wasim bowed his head. If he made this deathbed promise, he couldn't go back on his word. "I cannot make that decision for her."

"Wasim...convince her to marry soon." A rattling sound filled the back of King Khalid's throat.

Wasim quickly lifted his head and blinked back tears. "I will. We will be married soon." He tightened his fingers around his father's hand, as if by doing so he could keep the old man with him a little bit longer.

"I..." King Khalid's voice faded to a whisper, and Wasim watched the light dim in his eyes.

He leaned close to his father's ear and whispered, in a voice thick with sorrow, "I testify that there is no god but Allah, and Muhammad is the messenger of Allah."

THE PHONE RANG beside her bed, and Imani hopped up from the chair by the window and darted to it. She set down the novel she'd been using as a distraction ever since Wasim had called to tell her King Khalid had taken a turn for the worst.

Reluctantly, she set aside her glasses and picked up the phone. It was Wasim, and already her heart couldn't take the news she was certain he would convey.

"Hello?"

"Hello, Imani."

His voice sounded hoarse, and her heart broke into little pieces for him. Tears welled in her eyes.

"His Excellency King Khalid of the Kingdom of Barrakesch is no longer with us."

His pain reached across the line and snared Imani's heart in a tight fist. "I'm sorry, Wasim."

They knew this day was coming, yet it was still so unbearably painful. She was hurting so much because of her relationship with the king and his kindness to her. How much harder must it be for Wasim and the rest of the family to bear such a loss?

"*Subhanallah.*" Wasim spoke in the same pained voice.

"*Inna lillahi wa inna ilayhi raji'un,*" Imani whispered. "Call me if you need anything."

"I will."

They said their goodbyes, and Imani took a seat on the edge of the bed.

Doreen quietly entered and stood in the middle of the room, her dark eyes searching Imani's face. "Ambassador, is everything all right?"

"King Khalid has passed," Imani replied.

Doreen's eyes opened wide and her lips slightly parted. "Oh no." She covered her mouth with her left hand, and tears filled her eyes.

They had expected his death, but that didn't make the news any less devastating.

"When you speak to Prince Wasim again, please convey my condolences to him and his family."

"I will," Imani promised.

She heard the evening call to prayer through a loudspeaker from the minaret tower of the nearest mosque. The melodic sound had never been so haunting as it was right now, and heaviness filled her heart that the Barrakeschi people had lost their beloved leader today.

With King Khalid dead, Wasim would immediately ascend the throne and become the country's ruler. He would be very busy, not only taking on the role of king, but getting ready for the funeral. Burial would probably take place within the next twenty-four to forty-eight hours.

Imani called her family in Zamibia and gave them the news. Minutes later, she went downstairs to her home office and pulled out cards and stationery. Then she began the painful task of handwriting messages to members of the royal family expressing her condolences.

12

Imani entered the administrative offices of The Grand White Palace, but her steps faltered as she anticipated the conversation with Wasim. He'd asked her to come here for a meeting because, according to him, they needed to talk about "next steps" now that the mourning period was over.

Since women didn't attend funerals and burials, the last time she saw him was on television for the service over a week before. It had been a grand affair—if funerals could be called grand. With only twenty-four hours' notice, world leaders, mostly from Arab nations, came to pay their last respects to the great king. The day after, because King Khalid had presided over the armed forces, there had been a military salute and fighter planes flown overhead.

Talibah, who had been notified she was on her way up, approached when Imani stepped off the elevator in the outer office. Today she wore a dark brown abaya and vibrant red hijab accessorized with a lovely red and gold pin on the right side.

"Hello, Ambassador. How are you?"

"Fine, and you?"

Queen of Barrakesch   83

"Doing well, thank you. His Excellency is wrapping up a meeting. I've already told him you're here, so he shouldn't be much longer. Would you like something to drink while you wait—water, tea?"

At first, Imani had been taken aback by the honorific Talibah used, and then she remembered that Wasim was now king and had taken on the full title to go with his role as ruler.

"No, I'm fine. Thank you."

She sat on the sofa and while she waited, thumbed through emails she hadn't read yet. Only ten minutes later, two men dressed in suits came into the outer office, said a few words to Talibah, and then went on their way.

Talibah called back to Wasim, and after she hung up, smiled. "His Excellency will see you now," she said.

Imani took the long walk to his new office, the sound of her heels providing a gentle thump on the floor, which was covered in white tile edged with gold. The white walls were also painted with intricate gold designs that reached up to the high ceiling, and the combination of those colors made the entire place seem as if it glowed.

At the end of the hall, two men in traditional dress stood outside the double doors of Wasim's office. The gorgeous twenty-foot doors were made of a rich, dark wood where a local artist had carved scenes depicting ancient times in the country. At the very top, etched into the wall, was the image of a gold falcon, which appeared as if it was peering down at her as she approached.

Both men opened the doors simultaneously and Imani waltzed through. Wasim stood behind a massive wood desk that looked long enough to accommodate three people working behind it. His dark suit, dark tie and shirt, gave him a somber appearance that matched the grim expression on his face.

So much had changed. He was now king, and today they'd discuss how to bring their relationship to a close. She'd even thought of an idea on the way over. They could say that since he was caught up in the day-to-day responsibilities of being a new king, their relationship fell apart, which wasn't far-fetched.

"Imani," he said with a nod.

"Hello, Wasim."

The expression on his face was almost more than she could bear. There were tension lines around his mouth and a hint of hollowness in his eyes, as if he hadn't been sleeping well.

She walked over to the desk. "How are you?" she asked gently.

"I've been better." A brief smile crossed his lips.

"I hope you know that I'm here for you, if you need me. I've said that before, and I mean it."

"Thank you. That means a lot to me."

Wasim took a deep breath and appeared uncertain about how to proceed. Uncertainty was not an emotion she was used to seeing in him. She decided to help him along.

"I know you have important issues to take care of, so this conversation only has to take a few minutes. You were right to call this meeting because I'll only be in Barrakesch for a few more days, and the new ambassador arrives on Monday. What are your thoughts on how we should proceed with..." Imani glanced back at the open doors and lowered her voice. "Our relationship."

No emotion showed on his face. "I've thought about that a lot since my father died."

"And...how do you want to end this?" The words were more difficult to speak than she'd expected.

"Let's talk over here."

They walked along the expanse of the wall to the end where floor to ceiling windows overlooked the courtyard. Imani sat down, but Wasim remained standing.

"I have a proposition for you," he said.

"Okay," she said slowly.

He slipped one hand into his trouser pocket and walked slowly in front of the window. His profile was a study in deep concentration before he faced her again. "You saw how excited our families were when they learned we were ready for marriage. Everyone thinks we're compatible and a perfect match. And I agree. I think we should get married. To each other."

Imani let out a startled laughed. "What?"

His expression didn't change, which made her laughter seem completely out of place. She immediately sobered.

"Have you never thought about it? You and me? You can't deny there is something between us. We can build on that."

Imani's heart raced, and she licked suddenly dry lips. Had he really just offered her marriage? She didn't want to reveal how deeply attracted she was to him and the way he made her skin tingle without touching her.

That night in Estoria had upended her world in an unexpected way. She'd always had a bit of a crush on Wasim, but they'd only ever been friends. Good friends. She appreciated all his help when she had become the ambassador to their country. But what he was suggesting was outside the parameters of their friendship.

"Marriage is a serious undertaking. It shouldn't be entered into lightly, so sexual chemistry is not enough. We don't even know if we would enjoy each other."

"There's no doubt in my mind that we would enjoy each other," he said, eyes turning intense.

Imani felt that look as surely as if he'd touched her—wrapping his hand around her neck again and plowing her skin with kisses. The temperature in the room went up several notches, and she resettled on the sofa.

"I'm not Muslim, which would be a problem for the conservative members of your government. And I want to marry for love. You know that."

"And I have to get married."

He didn't have to tell her what was coming next. She already knew how royal families worked and the importance of having an heir to continue the family's lineage. She bent her head as unexpected pain twisted inside her at the thought of Wasim finding a wife and starting a family in the not-too-distant future.

She stood. "I came here today expecting you to tell me you've thought of a way for us to dissolve this fake engagement. You have what you wanted, your birthright. Your father chose you as his successor. There's no reason for us to be tied even more deeply together."

"I think a marriage could work between us."

"No."

A muscle in his hard jaw tightened. "You're not even going to consider it?"

"There's nothing to consider."

"Well then, we have a problem, because I promised my father you and I would get married right away."

He said the sentence so flippantly she gawked at him. "What!"

"You heard me."

"Pick someone else."

Wasim took a deep breath and ran a hand down his face. "I promised my father on his deathbed that I would marry *you*."

"And that's the only reason, because of a promise?" She swallowed the tightness in her throat but didn't wait for him to answer because she didn't want to hear him say *yes*. "I can't do it. We're not in love."

"Love can come later."

"That's your idea of a perfect marriage. Not mine."

"Would you have me disappoint my father?" he asked between gritted teeth.

"You made that promise, not me!" Imani hissed. "Getting

married was not part of the deal." She didn't want to be married to a man only to fulfill a promise to his dead father.

"Think about this. You would become the queen of an entire nation. You would have anything your heart desires, you only have to say the word and it would happen. Is that not better than your businessman?" He sneered the last sentence.

Imani's back went rigid. "We've already established that this marriage wouldn't work."

"You did, using religion as an excuse."

"That's a legitimate concern."

"Not for me."

"Because you're a king and wouldn't have to convert to another religion."

"I wouldn't require you to cover to Islam. We've already established that."

"Doesn't matter. I'm not interested." Imani folded her arms over her chest. This conversation had not gone at all how she had expected. "You're living in a fantasy world if you think a marriage between us could work. There are already rumblings from the conservative factions in the Parliament about us being together. They would be happy for us to split, and it would be a nightmare if we got married."

"As king, I have the power to dissolve the Parliament and start all over."

"That is a drastic, disruptive step, and you know it. The last time it was done was by your grandfather, and he did so to root out corruption."

His eyes flashed in annoyance. "Then believe this. You are a beloved ambassador from an allied nation. There are plenty of Zamibians living here that it's not so strange that you and I would marry. We've already established that we're engaged. One more step, and we'd be married. But there would be much more. A connection where our countries protected each other, exchanged ideas, promoted education together. Zamibia would have a foothold into the Gulf region, and we would have a foothold into Africa. Our partnership could strengthen our position on the world stage and protect our interests—economic and otherwise. This would be the perfect alliance between our countries."

Imani looked down at her fingers. His words wrecked her. To think she'd thought for one minute that he'd seen her as more than a friend. She couldn't consider his proposal. Not once had he mentioned having feelings for her, respecting her, cherishing her. Love was not a concern of his. All he cared about was an alliance and fulfilling a promise.

She looked him dead in his eyes. "A political alliance is not what I envisioned for my life. I'm sorry, I can't."

"I wish you would reconsider. We could make this work."

"No, we can't. To marry you would mean being in the worst kind of relationship I could imagine."

"The *worst*?"

"Yes. A loveless marriage with a powerful man. No, thank you." Imani's voice turned frigid. "You think that you can arrange a marriage and have it work out fine. I, on the other hand, find the old way distasteful. Romance, falling in love, courting—those are the things that I envision as part of my journey to marriage. If I can't have that, then I don't want it. I won't be tethered to someone, miserable, because we look good on paper. So now we're at a stalemate. How do you want to proceed with the dissolution of our relationship?"

His eyes turned icy. "I think we should wait. Until you've had time to think." He spoke with no inflection in his voice.

"There's nothing to think about. I've made my decision."

"Still, I'll give you time." He walked back toward the desk.

"I won't change my mind."

"If you say so."

"I mean it. Never."

"Never say never to me, *habibti*. You know how I love a challenge, and you know that I always win."

She glared at the back of his head and followed with her heels hitting the tile loud and strong. They both stopped at the desk, but he'd slipped a mask of emotionless calm on his features.

"I leave in three days," she whispered fiercely so the men outside couldn't hear.

"Then you have three days to reconsider," Wasim said coolly.

"You're already drunk with power." Imani stepped back. "Goodbye, Wasim. When you figure out how you want to end this, let me know." She stalked away.

"You'll change your mind," she heard him mutter.

She swung around and looked at him one more time, standing in front of the window in a three-piece suit, well-coiffed and confident. Wasim was a critical thinker. Behind the smiles and charm and gregarious personality was a ruthless negotiator who had expanded the wealth he'd inherited through the accumulation of real estate and other riches around the world. For a moment his confidence rattled her.

Then she straightened her spine, glared at him for good measure, and continued her power-walk out the door.

If he thought she'd change her mind about his ridiculous "offer," he had another think coming.

13

After Imani left, Wasim sat in his chair and stared at the closed doors.

Was the idea of marrying him so horrible? They knew each other. They had chemistry. They could both do worse.

Could there be another reason for her not wanting to marry him? Could she seriously be considering the man she'd told him about?

He picked up the phone and found the photo of the Senegalese man named Abdou. He'd had someone on his staff look him up. Well off but not wealthy, never married before, and a reputation of being kind. Imani knew this man and had chosen him over the other one her parents preferred.

Wasim's eyes rolled over his features. He was definitely handsome, looking more like a model than a businessman, with his high cheekbones and thick lips all covered in flawless ebony skin. Wasim tossed aside the phone.

He couldn't let Imani go. He'd made a promise, and besides, he wanted her. She was the ideal. The woman he'd been waiting for had been right in front of him all along. Now it was his job to show her that he was the man she'd been looking for.

The prince among the toads.

But that would take time. Until then, some arm-twisting would be required. She would hate him at first, but what he planned had to be done. Not only because of a promise to his father. Not only because their union created a powerful alliance, but because he'd tasted heaven on her lips.

Call it obsession, infatuation, compulsion—he didn't care about the label. All he knew was that Imani belonged with him, and he'd be damned if he let another man have her.

HANDS ON HER HIPS. Imani surveyed her downstairs office. The shelves were empty, and all of her office supplies and files were in boxes stacked around the room. After six years she was finally leaving Barrakesch for good.

Her heart was heavy, but she'd accomplished a lot and was proud of her record. She had shown that she was more than a pretty face. She had shown that being a woman did not limit her accomplishments to getting married and having a family.

The cultural exchange program she created between Barrakesch and Zamibia allowed young women the opportunity to live and work in either country for six months to a year by pairing them with roommates in the host country. The program fostered understanding across the cultures and provided work experience that could be used to gain employment in a variety of industries.

She had also created the women's trade initiative, which set aside a certain number of opportunities for women-owned Zamibian cottage industries, such as organic cosmetics made by hand and textile-making. That program was so successful that it went beyond Barrakesch's borders to include contacts she made in other Gulf states. And thanks to her cousin-in-law Dahlia, opportunities to sell looked promising in the United States, as well.

She'd worked on many more projects, but her greatest accomplishment was soon to come. She would be responsible for ironing out the details of the oil drilling project. A monumental deal that would add to the GDP of the Zamibian people for generations. By working with Barrakesch, they were able to keep most of the money inside the country instead of working with outsiders more interested in lining their own pockets. Billions of dollars in coming years—trillions! She couldn't count that high.

Imani strolled over to the desk and smoothed her fingertips over its empty surface. That all sounded great, except she hadn't yet heard from Wasim and worried that their confrontation could adversely affect the agreement. Surely he wouldn't cancel it altogether, but he could delay signing the contract out of anger.

King Khalid should have signed the agreement, but the delays with the environmental commission had pushed back the date, and now the contracts sat on Wasim's desk, the new king. The new king who was angry with her.

Surely he wouldn't let their disagreement keep him from signing it. After all, the joint venture benefited Barrakesch, too. They would receive a percentage of the oil revenues for a long time, simply for helping.

Her mobile phone rang and she picked it up. When she saw Yasmin's name, her face immediately broke into a smile.

"Hi, Yasmin," she said upon answering.

"Wasim told me you're leaving tomorrow. Is that true?" She sounded hurt.

"Yes, I'm going back to Zamibia. Remember, my post is up and the new ambassador arrives in a few days."

"I knew your post was up, but I assumed you'd stay since you and Wasim are getting married."

"Um, right now Wasim is busy getting settled into his role as king, and we haven't discussed a wedding date or made final plans yet."

Yasmin sighed. "Yes, he's very busy. I worry about the hours he's been putting in lately, but I know it must be done. As for the two of you, I hope you don't delay too long. I'm looking forward to having you as my sister-in-law. I want us to work together. Your enthusiasm for woman-focused projects are exactly what I need to help me with some of the charities I oversee. You and I could do a lot together, for both girls and women in the country."

Yasmin was a strong voice for women and children, and her work was not limited to Barrakesch. She was also a UNICEF regional ambassador who worked tirelessly on behalf of children's rights.

"Thank you, Yasmin." Her heart hurt a little bit at the thought that she wouldn't get to work on the projects with her because there would be no wedding.

"Keep in touch. Please," Yasmin said.

"I will. Take care, and thanks for calling."

Imani hung up the phone, feeling nostalgic and restless. She went out to the patio and recalled the last time she sat out there with Wasim. They'd shared dinner and talked about what they were looking for in a future spouse. Seemed like that conversation happened ages ago, but little more than a month had passed.

"Ambassador?"

Imani turned to face Vilma.

"A package arrived for you."

Imani reentered the office and took the envelope. "Thank you." As Vilma left, she tore it open.

When she saw the contents, her heart did a nosedive in her

chest. The letter was written on the official letterhead of the King of Barrakesch.

Subject: Oil drilling joint venture between the Kingdoms of Barrakesch and Zamibia.

Her fingers tightened on the trembling sheet when she read the first sentence of the first paragraph. *The project has been indefinitely delayed.*

"No," she whispered.

He'd done exactly what she'd feared.

14

The doors were barely opened before Imani swung through them and marched over to Wasim's desk. He didn't look up when she entered, as if he didn't hear her or know she was coming, when they both knew no one entered his offices without being announced first.

He continued writing with his head bent over some document. His indifference further inflamed her anger and she slammed the contract on the desk in front of him and received a small spurt of satisfaction when he jumped. He hadn't been expecting that.

"How dare you delay the signing!" she said.

"Lower. Your. Voice." His voice seethed with anger.

"I will not!" Imani slammed her hands on top of the contracts again. "We worked on this for over a year. All you have to do is sign it."

He tossed a dismissive glance at the papers and then met her gaze. "I'm a very busy man. I have other responsibilities now and don't have time to review those documents. When I have time, I will, but I don't know when that will be. Could be in three days, three months, or three years from now."

Imani straightened with her hands clenched at her sides. "You're despicable."

"Are you going to spend all day paying me compliments?"

"That wasn't a compliment, you ass." He arched a brow, and she immediately regretted the remark. She was here to get him to change his mind, and insulting him would probably not do that. She shifted tactic. "Kofi is your best friend and the Kingdom of Zamibia is depending on you to sign this agreement."

"The Kingdom of Zamibia delayed the process several times. I believe it is your environmental commission that put you in this tough spot. Besides, I'm sure Kofi will understand when he finds out I couldn't get to signing the agreement because my father just *died*. He will be disappointed but understanding, since the mourning period has only recently passed."

She felt a slight twinge of guilt when he pointed out that his father just died, but she quickly dismissed it because that was a false explanation and they both knew it.

"Is this you now? You'll be a fantastic king."

"Thank you. I look forward to a long rule."

She'd never seen him so dismissive of her feelings and while sarcasm and witty remarks had been common in their relationship, he'd never behaved like this with her before.

"This is beneath you, Wasim," Imani whispered, hoping to appeal to his softer side.

"Wanting to marry you is beneath me?" he asked sarcastically.

"Forcing my hand."

He lowered his voice. "Everyone expects us to get married."

She lowered her voice further. "But we agreed we wouldn't go that far. Marriage was not the endgame."

"The game has changed. My father is dead. On his deathbed, he asked me to marry you. All you have to do is say yes."

"Whether I want to or not? Forced marriages are forbidden in Islam."

"I am not forcing you to marry me. I offered you marriage, which you did not accept. According to my religion, which you love to toss in my face, we cannot be married without your consent. You do not give your consent, we cannot get married."

"That's twisted logic and you know it." She stepped back and let out several angry breaths in response to his uncaring, emotionless face. "I don't want to be stuck married to you."

"Stuck?" Wasim repeated, anger and affront evident in his voice and rigid posture.

"Spare me your indignation. I had much greater aspirations, and wanted more out of life than being the incubator for a man's royal seed."

His eyes narrowed. "I think you've insulted me enough for one day. If you did not come to give me the answer I want, then you can leave."

"Don't you believe in love at all? I do. I want to love the man that I marry."

"Then you will love me. You will give *me* your body *and* your heart."

"That's not how love works. But you don't care about any of that, do you? All you care about is winning. Wasim must always win, no matter the cost to his opponent. I wish I'd never agreed to this ridiculous farce of a relationship. Ironic, isn't it, that it was my idea?"

And now she was trapped, like a fly in a spider web, struggling and struggling to break free but not finding any way out. Because he held all the cards.

Wasim was good at reading people, finding their weakness and exploiting it. And he'd done that very thing to her. So much money was at stake. She couldn't allow the deal to fall apart when they were so close, and she couldn't allow it to be tabled indefinitely.

She was her father's only daughter and felt lost in a sea of testosterone and unquenchable need to prove herself and her capabilities. While her father never belittled her, she felt his condescension. That's why she'd worked so hard to demonstrate that she was as valuable as her brothers. All that would be taken away from her. Her biggest accomplishment.

And the women's programs she wanted to fund with proceeds from the oil revenues would fall by the wayside. More than a year of hard work down the drain, and all he had to do was sign his name.

"You know this project is important to me. You know about the women I'll be helping. Don't do this." She kept her voice strong and firm, refusing to beg though clearly at a disadvantage. She had her pride.

"I won't, if you marry me."

She'd didn't recognize the hard glint in his eyes. He was known to be a master negotiator, capable of wringing blood out of a turnip, but she'd never expected that skill to be turned on her.

Imani glared at him, wishing she could eviscerate him with only a look. But he was unmoving. How could she have ever thought she had feelings for him?

"I will never forgive you for this. Our relationship will never be the same." She leaned across the desk with one hand on its smooth surface. "Fine, Your Excellency, I'll marry you. But I will never love you."

He remained mostly unmoved, nonchalantly resting an elbow on the arm of his chair, only the narrowing of his eyes giving any indication that he heard what she'd said. "Well then, lucky for me, I don't need your love."

Their eyes locked in a battle of wills. Both stubborn. Both rigid.

Finally, Imani had had enough. With fire billowing through her veins, she swung around and left.

When she safely arrived downstairs, she blinked back tears of frustration as she fled the palace.

15

When Imani had returned to Zamibia, she arrived with one of Wasim's personal messengers, who hand-delivered the marriage contract to her parents. The negotiation had begun, listing details such as which country she and Wasim would reside in and their rights and responsibilities during the course of the marriage. It also included what Wasim would offer as her bridal gift, or *mahr*, valued in the millions and delivered over the course of several weeks after the *nikah* was signed.

Once the marriage contract was signed, Imani and Wasim were officially married, but Barrakeschi culture included a forty-day period between the signing and the announcement of the marriage to the world in a wedding ceremony. In keeping with tradition, she would remain separate from her husband and would stay in Zamibia during that period instead of moving into The Grand White Palace with him.

Imani sat in the living room of her father's apartment, pretending not to notice that Kofi was staring her. Her cousin was a suspicious man and saw her as his little sister, and she was certain they'd have a private conversation soon.

Until then, she listened to her father and mother's excited chatter as they reviewed the document. Benu had been hesitant at first, unaccustomed to the idea of a marriage contract, but Prince Kehinde had expressed no hesitation.

He was excited about her becoming the queen of a nation and that she would be the one to unite the two countries, which could prove profitable for generations to come. Their natural resources would be shared. Their militaries would learn from and support each other. Travel between both countries would become even easier, allowing the smooth flow of ideas and innovations, goods and services, and a mingling of cultures.

At the end of the conversation, Imani left the room and went to her personal suite in her father's living quarters. She didn't pay attention to the opulent room that had been hers for years. She sat down in front of the window, propped her feet on a table, and stared out at the grounds. Numb.

She was being treated as nothing more than a commodity in this whole transaction. Her worst nightmare had come true. Under different circumstances she would have been happy about this marriage. But she didn't only want marriage. She wanted love and respect, too.

One out of three isn't bad, she thought bitterly.

At the loud sound of rapping knuckles, she swung her head toward the door. "Come in."

Kofi entered, striding across the carpeted floor, his concerned gaze trapping hers. He looked particularly well-groomed today because earlier he'd received a haircut and his circle beard had been freshly trimmed.

"Hi, Kofi. To what do I owe this visit?" Imani put as much of an upbeat sound in her voice as she could and went the extra mile of smiling.

"What is going on?"

"What do you mean?" She stood and put a confused frown on her face, though she knew exactly what he meant.

"You're really going to marry Wasim?"

"You've known that was a possibility for some time. Since before King Khalid passed."

His eyes scoured her features. "I want to be happy for you, but this doesn't feel right to me. Your entire relationship hasn't felt right from the beginning, but I held my tongue."

"What do you think? That Wasim seduced me?" Imani asked, purposely making light of the situation with a slight smirk.

Kofi did not see the humor in the situation and his face remained serious. "Granted, I noticed there was an attraction between the two of you, but you've dated a number of men over the years, and though I realize they haven't been love matches, not once did you ever mention Wasim as a potential husband. This feels more like an arranged marriage, and I distinctly remember you telling me you wanted to marry for love."

Momentarily, she turned her back to him, allowing time for her to think of an answer. When she turned to him, her face was schooled into neutral lines that didn't gave away an inkling of the emotional turmoil she suffered under.

"As you pointed out, none of my previous relationships were love matches. In this case, I know Wasim. I know Barrakesch. An alliance between our countries makes sense, and I will be a part of it."

He shook his head. "None of this makes sense. An alliance, perhaps. But not with you."

"Then who? You don't have any sisters, and I'm my father's only daughter."

He still looked doubtful. She hadn't convinced him. He took slow steps over to where she stood and looked down into her face. His eyebrows lowered into a deep V over his eyes. "Are you sure? If you don't want to do this..."

"Are you crazy? How can I not? It will be my greatest accomplishment. Wasim and I will go down in history."

Kofi rested his hands on her shoulders and looked deeply into her eyes. Then he spoke in his quiet, intense way. "This is more than history. This is more than an accomplishment, Imani. You remember how miserable my first wife, Azireh, was when we married? I don't want the same fate for you."

Royal liaisons were often built around practicality instead of love, and his first marriage had been such a union, which ended in disaster.

"I won't kill myself, if that's what you're worried about. Your marriage was arranged, and Azireh was in love with someone else. I am not."

"There is no one else you love and wish to marry?"

That question she could answer honestly. "No, there isn't."

He nodded, seeming satisfied with that answer, and dropped his hands from her shoulders. "If you ever change your mind about going down in history, will you let me know?"

She nodded. "But I won't."

Kofi pulled her into his arms, and she rested her cheek against his chest. She inhaled a quiet, shaky breath. Unlike her father, he expressed concern and wanted to make sure she was happy. It was her job to convince him their marriage would be real, because if she gave the slightest indication that she wasn't happy or was entering into this marriage with any hesitation, he would ask his father to override her father's decision to give consent to the marriage. Because Kofi saw her as a whole human being.

Dahlia was lucky to have him as a husband. He supported her in a way that she longed to experience from her father but never had.

Kofi pulled away. "I'll see you later for dinner."

Imani nodded, unable to use her voice when emotions threatened to overwhelm her.

Kofi walked away without another word, but she knew her cousin.

"Kofi."

He turned.

"Promise me something."

He frowned. "Anything."

"Promise me you won't confront Wasim."

His face hardened.

"Please. Promise me."

At first she thought he wouldn't. The time between her request and his answer lengthened into an uncomfortable silence.

Finally he said, with great gravity in his voice, "I promise."

When he left the room, Imani collapsed onto a chair. That was it.

It was only a matter of time before the marriage contract was signed, and she became Wasim's wife.

16

Only three days left.

The forty-day waiting period was almost over, and Imani was back in Barrakesch.

She perused the crowded room from a seated position near the back. There were no less than seventy-five women in attendance, some she knew and some she didn't. Dahlia and Angela were there and so were Yasmin and Wasim's other sisters. Benu, her father's two other wives, cousins, and friends from both Barrakesch and Zamibia had all come together for her henna party.

Tonight she felt like a queen because her chair looked like a throne and she sat on a raised platform. The seat was covered in bright red velvety fabric and gold tassels edged its bottom. Her bare feet rested on a matching ottoman, and her arms on armrests painted gold. The gold extended to the feet of the chair as well as framed the red at her back.

She remained very still, because on either side of her, attendants drew patterns on her skin. By the end of the night, her hands and feet would be covered in henna designs that symbolized joy, blessings for a happy marriage, and fertility.

She'd spent the thirty-seven days prior making plans for the move to Barrakesch. Her father had spoken to her Ghanaian suitor soon after the signing of the *nikah* and informed him that she was no longer a potential wife. She heard he hadn't been happy, but no doubt he'd find himself another potential wife very soon.

In addition to getting ready for the move, she'd made preparations for the wedding. Wasim had sent a team of women to The Grand Palace of Zamibia to prepare her according to Islamic and Barrakeschi customs. In conjunction with her usual aides, they made sure she ate well, bathed in the purest water, and every day was rubbed down with organic oils and scented lotions that ensured her skin and hair were glowing and soft.

During the same period, Wasim had sent the bridal gifts to Zamibia. The gifts were extravagant and her property alone. Per tradition, they ensured a woman's financial security in the event she and her husband divorced or she became widowed. According to the terms of the *nikah*, he sent jewelry worth in the millions—necklaces with diamonds, rubies, and emeralds, along with their matching earrings and bracelets. Over a dozen rings that also contained diamonds, blue sapphires, and other precious stones. Gold combs for her hair, and a particularly stunning ankle bracelet made of platinum with a round emerald in its center.

Then there was the deed to a building in Manhattan and another to land in the French countryside. Beautiful silk fabrics, as well as a collection of European art, including an original Van Gogh. The final gift came in the amount of a lump sum deposit of millions of dollars into her personal account.

In recent days, her initial anger had melted away and transformed into nervous anticipation. Anticipation of her responsibilities as queen, but also anticipation of her wedding night. She and Wasim had only shared a kiss so far, but it had been explosive, and her thoughts veered toward anxiety and desire every time she considered sharing a bed with him.

But spending time with her mother and friends had been what she needed. Having so many people around her during this period lifted her spirits, despite the circumstances surrounding her marriage.

Three additional henna artists worked the room by putting designs on the hands of the guests. A female DJ played a mix of music, from Middle Eastern sounds to West African beats. The women danced around each other, laughing and talking.

Gifts for the guests were lined up at a table near the front. Attendants would hand them out as the women left. Each velvet drawstring pouch contained perfume, organic soaps, and Zamibian candy made from mangoes and pineapples that she'd had specially made for the occasion.

Plenty of food and drink filled the tables lining the walls, representing a blend of both cultures. Snacks like chin chin, plantain chips, meat pies, and candied nuts all made according to Zamibian tradition. Then there was grilled avocado salad, hummus served with vegetables and pita bread, and *kanafeh*—a sticky pastry she'd become quite fond of.

Hours later, her hands and feet were covered in the intricate patterns created by the artists, and the reddish-brown stain would darken over the course of the next couple of days.

Someone hugged her from behind, and she knew right away it was Dahlia. "How are you?"

Imani turned to face her cousin's wife and saw Angela, Dahlia's best friend and Prince Andres's wife, standing there, too.

Angela wore very little makeup on her amber skin and had fixed her hair into a loose chignon. Dahlia wore her long wavy hair in a single braid over one shoulder. Her dark skin and dark eyes seemed to glow under the lights overhead.

"I'm good," Imani replied.

"Glad to hear it. Kofi told me to keep an eye on you and report back." Dahlia raised an eyebrow in question.

Imani sighed. He was ridiculously protective, and she loved him. "Tell him there is nothing to report."

Dahlia's face turned into an affectionate smile. "I'm so happy for you."

"We both are," Angela said.

"You deserve this, Imani. You've worked so hard all these years, and I knew from the moment I saw you and Wasim together, that you were meant to be. You had too much chemistry. Anyone with two working eyes could see that the two of you were interested in each other and belong together."

Belonged together? Imani wasn't so sure about that, but she couldn't tell Dahlia what she saw had not been real. That they had simply been two friends flirting and getting along, but after the kiss, the flirtations became something more. And only recently did she admit that she had feelings for Wasim, but he had crushed her spirits when he told her the reasons they should get married.

Dahlia placed an arm around her shoulders. "Come on, we need to dance."

Imani let both women lead her into the middle of the group and joined in the dancing.

THE WEDDING CEREMONY was a large affair that included almost a thousand attendees. The men's celebration took place in a large hall of the palace, while the women's celebration took place in an even larger room. In addition to the many friends and family that were invited, celebrities and dignitaries from around the world came to take part in the celebration. In the male hall, all of the men dressed in traditional white robes and the nation's standard headdress.

Wasim looked at the number of men gathered to help him celebrate. Though he and Imani had been officially married for forty days, tonight marked the moment when they could celebrate with the rest of the world. He felt lighter than he had in a long time and glad that he had waited instead of accepting the choices his aunt had presented to him over the years.

He moved from person to person and smiled at the guests, but could barely concentrate. It seemed like he had waited an eternity for this night, and now that it was here, he wished he could kick everyone out of the palace and take his wife upstairs and make love to her until the early morning. Unfortunately, he had to be a good host and a proper groom.

He spotted Andres and Kofi chatting over near one of the tables and sauntered over to them.

Andres's blue eyes lit up. "Did you invite enough people?" he asked.

"You're a fine one to talk. When you and Angela got married, not only did an entire country attend, I seem to recall there were news cameras that broadcast the event to the entire world."

"He does have a point," Kofi said.

"Touché," Andres said. "You know, I actually thought you would back out of the marriage, but I was wrong."

"Why did you think that?"

"Because you've found something wrong with every woman your aunt presented to you and made it quite plain that you didn't want to get married anytime soon."

"Things changed." Wasim shrugged.

"Welcome to the married men's club."

"Honored to be a member," Wasim said.

"I'm sorry your father couldn't be here."

"Me too," Kofi added quietly.

Pain bloomed in his chest. "I wish he could have been here,

too, but I like to think he knows that Imani and I are married, which was what he wanted."

Music started playing, a traditional tune on a flute and drums, with the voices of a chorus of men joining in. Then attendants began handing out bamboo canes to all the guests.

"What's this for?" Kofi asked.

Wasim smiled. "This is our traditional stick dance—Al Ayala. Watch and learn."

The stick dance was a tradition that was being revitalized after the younger people had not expressed much interest in it. The cultural minister had been worried that the art would be lost, and so in the past, Wasim had allocated funds from his own budget to promote it in schools and cultural centers around the city.

The men lined up facing each other, and Wasim slipped into place between one of his cousins and Akmal. Moving in time to the chanting voices of the chorus, Wasim joined the guests as they lifted the canes high and then lowered them again. They moved in coordinated movements that had been honed through years of practice.

After a while, he glanced at his friends. "Come on, join in," he told them.

He couldn't be with his new bride yet, but he could have fun with his best friends and perhaps forget for a moment that there would be several more hours before the night ended and he and Imani could be alone.

Andres and Kofi stepped into the line and quickly caught on to the movements. Wasim tossed his spinning cane in the air and caught it, which prompted Akmal to do the same. Then the two brothers started doing other tricks as they moved in time to the sound of the beating drums and the chant of the male voices around them.

They twirled their canes, tossed them high, and caught them with ease. Youthful and exuberant, Akmal dropped low while twirling and then came back up again. With a hearty laugh, Wasim did, too. He and his brother were soon joined by several other participants who could do tricks, and the five men put on a show.

Later, at the appointed time, Wasim and the men he chose —his brothers, Prince Kehinde, Imani's six brothers, Farouk, Andres, and Kofi—headed toward the room where the women celebrated. He hadn't seen Imani in forty days. Impatiently, he waited outside while the women who guarded the door announced that the men had arrived so that the women who preferred to cover their heads in a man's presence could put back on their scarfs.

Wasim entered first and he ignored every other woman, gaze landing immediately on Imani.

His breath caught. She was stunning.

She'd chosen not to wear the typical white gown that Barrakeschi brides preferred. Instead, she wore a silk dress from Zamibia, a loose-fitting white gown trimmed in gold lace that draped over her curves in a complimentary way. The rounded neckline allowed her to display numerous gold necklaces and though the sleeves were long, he could clearly see the henna pattern on her hands and the string of gold bracelets that decorated her wrists. Her hair was covered in a white and gold head covering that matched the dress. Gold lipstick and dots below her eyes in gold face paint completed the look.

Wasim's chest grew tight as his gaze remained on his wife. He barely heard the applause and sounds of ululation from the women who surrounded her. She was even more beautiful than he expected.

Selfishly, despite the problems between them, he knew he'd made the right decision.

And tonight he'd do everything he'd wanted to do to her ever since she stepped off the plane from Zamibia six years ago.

17

Outside the sound of fireworks over the harbor cracked like gunshots in the night and marked the end of the celebration of Imani's and Wasim's wedding ceremony.

Inside, Imani stood at the side of the bed in her apartment, taking deep breaths to calm her racing pulse. She hadn't been with a man in so long she wondered if she remembered how to have sex. A few minutes ago, the maids had left after cleansing her skin, washing her face, and styling her hair, and very soon Wasim would be coming down the hall from his apartment.

Her king-sized bed was filled with fluffy pillows and covered in simple white linens, a striking contrast to the rest of the bedroom's luxurious gold and cream decor. Above her, a wide and deep recessed ceiling with a heavy chandelier showered bright light over the room, and on either side of the headboard rested ceiling-high mirrors with an etched design. A cream European-style dresser sat against the opposite wall with a large bouquet of red roses in a vase, while its matching tables sandwiched the bed.

The complete suite included a bathroom and another room

that opened through an arched doorway where she could sit and have breakfast or read in the evenings. The room was lovely and the furnishings elaborate, but they weren't enough to make her forget that tonight was her wedding night.

She heard the door snick open and then close, and her muscles bunched with tension. The light overhead went out and only the pale golden glow from one of the lamps on the bedside tables illuminated the room.

Behind her, Wasim didn't say a word, and she had the sudden urge to cover her body and hide the lavender silk and lace nightie that barely covered her ass and left little to the imagination.

Imani faced her husband. "Came to claim your marital rights?"

"If you think by talking to me like that you'll turn me away, you're mistaken."

"Can't blame me for trying."

"I'm not a monster, Imani."

"So I imagined everything that took place over the past couple of months?"

With deliberate slowness Wasim came toward her and stopped inches away. The earthy fragrance of his cologne and the underlying scent of oud drifted into her nostrils.

As he dipped his head, his lips grazed her hair and his breath brushed her earlobe. "Do you remember that night in Estoria? You have no idea how difficult it was to stop kissing you. I have craved you for so long, and tonight I won't stop. Tonight..." He kissed behind her ear and the textured softness of his beard added another dimension of sensation. "Tonight I will know every inch of you."

She turned away and tried to fight her response to his closeness, his scent, his virility as he towered over her. But Wasim placed a hand at the back of her neck and pulled her into a crushing kiss.

Her senses went into an uproar as threads of heat raced through her body. That night, that kiss, and all contact since then had placed a constant strain on her willpower. Now she was free to give in, and she needed more.

Imani wanted to press her aching nipples against his chest to ease the sexual irritation caused by his kisses, but Wasim refused. He held her at bay. In the midst of plundering her mouth, he somehow managed to maintain control while she was on the verge of performing a lewd grind against his hips.

When he tore his lips from hers, Imani gasped in frustration.

"Show me," he rasped, taking one of her wrists and scouring the henna designs.

She knew immediately what he wanted to see.

"Here," Imani said quietly, pointing to her inner forearm where his name was hidden in the pattern. "And here." The other artist had hidden his name in the same spot on her left forearm.

He whispered something she didn't understand and then kissed her again, hard and long. When he finally stopped, he stripped out of his clothes, and Imani's mouth went dry.

For years she'd only had her imagination for an idea of what Wasim must look like underneath his clothes, but her mind had fallen far short of the reality. His classic male physique consisted of sculpted muscles that ran the length of his body from shoulders to calves. His athletic build made her want to reach out and stroke his firm chest, run her fingers down his flat belly, or squeeze the muscles that bulged from his thighs. Wisps of dark hair trailed from his chest to his pelvis and made a path down his legs.

He moved closer, oozing sexual energy and masculine grace. "Your turn."

Within seconds he'd removed her clothes and was on top of her on the bed.

To think, she'd planned to lie there on the mattress as an unwilling participant, but that thought had been quickly dismissed the moment he kissed her. Hunger battered her loins and she kissed Wasim with all the pent-up desire that had banked over time.

When his fingers slipped between her lower lips, she twisted in shock.

"You're already so wet. You burn for this as much as I do," he groaned against her collarbone.

She succumbed to the battering ram of his seduction, gripping his powerful shoulders and twisting her head to claim his mouth. She sucked on his bottom lip and thrust her tongue between his lips.

He became almost brutal as he devoured her and matched her ardor. He stretched her hands above her head and clamped her wrists together with one hand. Then his tongue whisked over the tip of one breast while the other bore the brunt of his hand's fondling. He squeezed and kneaded and dragged his thumb across the turgid nipple until she was arching her back and writhing in the sheets.

Wasim went lower, alternating between kisses and whispering erotic words against her skin. "Do you know how many times I've dreamed about this night? How many times I've imagined you naked?"

He slid his hands beneath her, and his fingers pressed into her bottom as he lifted her to his face. His mouth covered her wet, feminine flesh, and her head fell back. She grabbed the pillows as she lost her bearing, dizzy with pleasure as his lips and tongue devoured her with relish, like a man under the harsh lash of starvation.

With one heel propped against his shoulder and fingers gripping a handful of his hair, Imani gasped and whimpered, leaving her legs open so he could take what he wanted from between her quivering thighs.

She came only moments later and trembled through an earth-shattering orgasm. Wasim cradled her body in his arms and waited until her breathing was back to normal before he resumed his exploration.

He truly did learn every inch of her—back, front, thighs, arms, breasts. Not one square inch remained untouched as they made love. He sank his fingers into her hair and brushed his hands over her curves. Gathering her breasts in his hands and sucking her swollen nipples, he made her desire heat up once again to boiling.

She wanted him so badly the aching spot between her legs grew wetter every time his hair-roughened thigh brushed against her tender flesh. She bit her lips to resist the urge to beg but didn't know how long that would last if he didn't take her soon.

As if he heard her silent plea, Wasim shifted. Gripping his erection, he looked at her with darkened eyes, his face intent. He settled over her on one arm and brought the broad head of his erection to kiss the entrance of her body.

As he sank into her, she shifted her hips up and absorbed the slide of his hard length. She almost wept, shuttering her eyes as he took full possession of her body. Groaning, her mouth open, Imani shuddered.

"You're so tight. So wet." Wasim let out a helpless groan.

Then his hips were in motion—slowly at first as they got accustomed to each other, but then he increased his speed. The mattress groaned under the weight of his forceful thrusts, and her body arched higher. He whispered sensual words to her in Arabic, telling her how soft her skin was and how good it felt to be inside her.

"You're mine now," he whispered.

Her eyes flew open.

He seized her mouth and she became filled in two places.

Her arms went around his neck, gripping him close while

he sucked her ear and her neck, never once losing the in-and-out rhythm.

Imani guided the fingers of one hand into his thick hair, and then she was airborne, shuddering through another climax that rocked her with the force of an earthquake. As Wasim's heated grunts beat against her throat, her pulsing cries bounced off the walls. She had never experienced this with any other man. It was surreal. She moved her hips in a frenzy of motion so she wouldn't miss a single one of his pleasure-giving thrusts.

In the middle of her orgasm, Imani achieved some clarity. She hated clarity and wished she could go back to not knowing —not knowing that she loved him and all this time she'd been in deep denial. The truth was a terrible burden to carry in a marriage of convenience based solely on a promise and a political pact.

She curled her fingers into tight fists at the back of his head and silently responded to what he'd said.

Yes, I'm yours.

IMANI GLANCED OVER AT WASIM. She thought he'd go back to his apartment, but he lay very still on his back. Within minutes, she heard him breathing evenly.

In the glimmer of the lamp beside the bed, his skin was golden. Her eyes trailed over his tousled hair, the neatly groomed beard on his face that had gently scraped between her breasts and along her inner thighs, the sprinkling of dark hair on his chest, and the sculpted muscles that defined his arms and abdomen.

She rolled away from him and squeezed her eyes shut. She had never had *this*—this type of passion before. Either she'd gone without sex for so long she'd forgotten how good it could be, or that was literally the best sex she'd ever had. Her nerves still hadn't calmed down. They clamored for more contact—rough, gentle—any way he chose to touch her.

She turned off the lamp, tugged the sheet over her nakedness, and prayed for sleep. She didn't want to dwell on what she'd just learned. Loving him was foolish, and she was no fool. She knew better.

Eventually sleep arrived but was abruptly disrupted when Wasim's hands caressed her body in the middle of the night. He reawakened her desire with gentle kisses on her breasts and sucking her nipples into his mouth and letting his tongue play with the tender peaks. His fingers moving between her legs and stroking her inner thighs made her wet and horny and she arched feverishly into his touch.

Her jagged breathing met his hungry groans and then Wasim pushed her legs apart and joined their bodies with one smooth thrust. Very little foreplay was needed because she was as wet as he was hard.

He pulled her on top of him and with his hands on her waist, he let her ride. Imani tossed back her head, the sounds of her sexual enjoyment coming out as sharp cries that filled the room. It didn't take long for them to climax, and afterward she collapsed on top of him.

Their heavy breaths bathed each other's heated skin as they came down off their high. Wasim shifted so that she was cradled against his chest, and he flung an arm over her waist.

As Imani closed her eyes, she marveled at how much making love to Wasim had impacted her already. She didn't feel like herself. She felt reborn.

Drifting off to sleep, she knew twice in one night was not going to be enough for Wasim, because it was nowhere near enough for her.

I mani squinted into the sunlight coming in through the large windows of her bedroom. The heavy drapes that effectively blocked out all the light had been pulled aside by one of the maids.

"Good morning, Your Highness." She looked older than Imani, perhaps in her forties.

Imani groaned, closed her eyes, and rolled over into the soft, fluffy pillows. Wasim had left her bed at some point last night, but his scent remained. It clung to the sheets, so much so that she almost felt him, as if he hadn't left the bed.

"His Excellency requests your presence at breakfast this morning," the maid said.

Imani opened her eyes to respond and was startled to see another maid, a younger one, standing quietly with her hands clasped in front of her. Being a member of the royal family of Zamibia, she was accustomed to having servants around. But she hadn't been a princess or queen and had only been assigned one morning maid, so seeing two was unusual for her.

"What time is it?" she mumbled.

The older maid answered. "Seven-fifteen. His Excellency requests your presence at eight o'clock."

Well, His Excellency can kiss my ass, Imani thought obstinately. He'd kept her up half the night and now wanted her at an early morning breakfast. How ridiculous.

She pulled the linens over her shoulders and settled deeper against the pillows. "I won't be able to make breakfast at that time. However, I would like breakfast in my room later, at ten o'clock, please."

Imani closed her eyes, having every intention of going back to sleep and getting some much needed additional rest. The soreness in her aching limbs was a painful reminder that she'd been abstinent for several years. In a couple more hours, she'd be in better shape to face the day.

However, the odd silence made her open one eye. The two maids stood uncertainly in the room. The younger one looked nervously at the older one, and Imani sighed internally. She may be the queen, but Wasim was the king, and he had given them instructions which she was now contradicting. It wasn't fair to put them in such a tough position.

Sitting up and holding the sheet against her naked chest, she smiled. "I'm kidding. Please run me a bath, and what were your names again?"

Relieved smiles covered the women's faces, and they gave their names. While the older one went to prepare her bath, Imani gave the younger one instructions on which clothing items she wanted to wear to breakfast. The young woman went off to the huge walk-in closet to get the items.

Imani sat back against the pillows and reflected on when Wasim left her bed in the early morning. She should have been relieved, but a twinge of pain had blossomed over her left breast as she lay there in the dark.

His name might be written on her skin, and she might be

wearing a diamond and platinum ring that proclaimed her as his wife, but she had been left very much alone.

At five minutes after eight, Imani walked out onto a glass-enclosed balcony where Wasim sat at a table sipping on a cup of coffee and reading an electronic tablet. Probably the financial news, as he stayed abreast of changes in the stock market around the world so that he could make better decisions about the royal family's investments.

When she approached, he looked pointedly at the watch on his wrist and then quickly assessed her appearance. She wore a long-sleeved orange tunic that reached her knees and cream, wide-legged pants underneath. She hadn't had time to do much with her hair, so she kept it simple, wearing it straight and tucking the right side behind her ear while allowing the left side to swoop across her left brow.

She thought she was simply dressed, but Wasim looked at her with such hunger she was almost embarrassed, certain the servants that hovered nearby could see how much he wanted her. His gaze lingered on her lips, still slightly swollen from his amorous kisses the night before, and she quickly took her seat because the intensity of his stare made her legs unsteady.

His power over her was nerve-racking. The smart, independent, strong-willed woman she considered herself had become foolish, dependent, and weak overnight. She hated him and loved him. He angered her but made her hunger for him, too. Nothing made sense anymore, so she'd concentrate on what was safe and would protect her from harm.

Anger. Anger was her shield.

Imani cleared her throat. "I was told that you wanted me...I mean, requested my presence at breakfast. Was there any particular reason for that?" She draped a white napkin over her thighs.

"I wanted to tell you about my plans," Wasim replied. He extended his cup and one of the male servers refilled it with coffee. "But before we get started, let's order breakfast."

They placed their breakfast orders, and when Imani also had a cup of coffee in front of her, Wasim dismissed the servers so they were alone on the balcony. She'd never been out here before, and the view was spectacular. She could see the harbor with sailboats, yachts, and the largest yacht, which belonged to the royal family. A heliport with two helicopters was also visible from here.

Wasim set down his tablet and gave her his undivided attention. "I'm going to loan you a few members of my staff. They'll help you get oriented with areas of the palace you weren't privy to before we married and help you get acquainted with the rest of the employees that work for us. You'll also need to start putting together your own staff, and I'm sure I don't have to tell you about the employment requirements."

"No, you don't."

Barrakeschi law required that for any entity that employed more than fifty employees, at least twenty-five percent of them must be a citizen of Barrakesch. This ensured job security for Barrakeschis in a country with a large expat population and ensured that wages stayed stable.

The kingdom also maintained a prominent presence in another part of the business sector. They required a twenty-five percent stake in any foreign company they granted the permission of being allowed to operate on their soil. This generated additional income for the royal family and funded programs that benefited the population as a whole.

Imani and Wasim discussed other operational issues surrounding the residential areas of the palace and timelines for completion. While they talked, their meals arrived. Imani listened to Wasim's suggestions as she ate spicy scrambled eggs and waffles doused in maple syrup, and he consumed boiled eggs, cheese, bread, and tahini with molasses.

The entire conversation was cool and very civilized, like two business people discussing contracts rather than newlyweds talking about how to merge their households and manage their responsibilities as a highly visible royal couple.

While she agreed with Wasim that love before marriage could work—she'd seen it work many times herself in the arranged marriages in her country as well as here—there was no guarantee. She'd wanted affection, love, and respect to preclude any marriage. Instead, she was seated on a balcony sipping coffee, staring out at the azure blue of the Gulf while her husband returned his attention to the electronic tablet in front of him now that their conversation was over.

"Was there anything else?" Imani asked tartly, to get his attention.

Wasim looked up from the tablet with a frown between his eyes. He clearly didn't appreciate the interruption.

"No, unless you have a question."

"No questions. I'll get right to work." She pushed back the chair, tossed the napkin on top of the table, and stood.

His eyes followed her movement, and he opened his mouth to say something, but she walked away. She didn't care what he had to say. Her misery was palpable.

This was exactly the kind of chilly relationship she'd promised herself she'd never have—yet here she was.

19

S ince their wedding night, Wasim had returned to the business of running the country. Caught up in meetings much of the day, he didn't communicate very often with Imani except to meet for dinner, make love, and then go back to his apartment afterward. She should be glad that he left her alone and only bothered her when he needed her to fulfill her duty as his wife. After all, she had plenty to keep her busy. Learning the palace norms, meeting with her own staff, and getting up to date on the programs and causes she could champion and work on with the princesses, or on her own as queen.

But she wasn't happy. She felt...neglected. Though she was loath to admit it, she wanted Wasim's attention outside of sex and the occasional meal.

Rather than betray those feelings, she concentrated on learning all she could about the various projects available for her to work on. The ones that appealed to her the most involved women and girls, and she focused her energy on expanding those initiatives.

She and Yasmin met one morning to discuss a passion project for Yasmin—a literacy program in rural areas that had slowly grown over the years. Though the country had a high standard of living and low crime, illiteracy was high among the people in the rural areas, particularly the girls and women. During King Khalid's reign, Yasmin had convinced her father to send teachers to those remote areas because logistically it was difficult to have them come regularly to the city for classes. Eventually, she hoped to build more girl schools to help with the problem.

Imani loved to read. Reading had opened up a whole world to her as a child, so Yasmin's project was exactly the kind of thing she could get excited about. They both sat on the sofa in Imani's office discussing a trip to the rural areas. Yasmin wanted Imani to observe the work she'd done and consider promoting the project by convincing Wasim to instruct Parliament to increase the budget so she could expand the program.

"Have you asked Wasim already?" Imani asked.

"He's busy, and he'll want to see facts and figures that I don't have. How can you quantify the changes made in these women's lives? In the lives of their families because they can now read. They can take the bus into the city on their own and order supplies for their households without having to wait for their husbands or sons to do it for them. And the daughters get to see their mothers becoming more independent and learn from their example."

She spoke so passionately that Imani was immediately intrigued. These were exactly the kinds of projects she worked on in Zamibia, and she would love to do the same in Barrakesch.

"When can we go to see the recipients of the program?"

"As soon as you like," Yasmin said immediately.

"How about day after tomorrow?"

"Yes, absolutely! Since we'll be gone most of the day, I will check with Farouk to make sure that works for him." She immediately fired off a text, and the answer came back right away. A big grin spread on her face. "Day after tomorrow is no problem. Farouk will take Malak to the worksite with him. He loves to do that, and put on a hard hat like his father and the other men."

"Good. We're all set."

"Um, do you need to check with Wasim?"

"No. He's busy during the day, so I'm sure it's no problem."

"I see," Yasmin said, her voice filled with doubt.

Imani quickly added, "But I'll mention it tonight when I see him at dinner." No point in letting her sister-in-law know there was tension between them.

Yasmin's face transformed into a smile. "If anything changes, let me know."

NOTHING CHANGED.

The next morning, Imani woke up in bed alone, again. Wasim hadn't come to her room the night before, nor had he eaten dinner with her, so she'd eaten alone and then called her mother and Dahlia to chat. Afterward, she reviewed the details of the literacy program, and Wasim called to tell her that he had an early flight in the morning to attend a two-day summit in Pakistan.

That was it. He didn't ask about her plans, and she didn't tell him she would be leaving to go into the countryside.

She ate breakfast with Wasim's sisters and their mother on the fourth floor and was in her office getting ready to meet Yasmin downstairs when a package arrived from Wasim's office. She thanked the courier and walked over to her desk. She pulled out the sheets of paper and saw red.

It was the agreement between Barrakesch and Zamibia.

Imani flipped through the pages. They were copies, but in all the places across from King Babatunde's signature, Wasim had signed his own name and applied the royal seal. Dated yesterday. No doubt a set of originals were in his office and another set on the way to Zamibia.

A maelstrom of emotions seized her, and tears sprang to her eyes. Finally, the project she'd worked so hard on would come to fruition. But a hint of bitterness underlay the joy. That he'd been so dismissive of such an important moment rubbed her the wrong way. That she was here, in the palace because he'd withheld this very document, hanging it over her head in exchange for her agreement to marry him.

Imani tossed the papers to the desk and called Wasim. After two rings, he answered his personal phone.

"Hello?" he said, sounding distracted.

She heard voices in the background. "Hello, Wasim. I received the signed agreement a few minutes ago."

"Good. I'm sure you're pleased." He whispered something to someone nearby. He wasn't even giving her his full attention.

"I am pleased. Ecstatic," she said in a caustic tone.

Pause.

"Are you?" he asked cautiously.

"Of course. You gave me what I wanted. Finally. *Shukraan.* When will you be returning from your trip?"

"Day after tomorrow."

"Okay. Well, maybe I won't be here when you get back."

"*Excuse me?*"

"I said, I might not be here when you get back. I have what I wanted now."

Wasim didn't say a word. He didn't make a sound. She couldn't even hear him breathe. All she heard were the voices of men speaking in the background.

Finally, he said, in a steely voice, "Hold for one moment, please."

Seconds later, he covered the mouthpiece and had a muffled conversation.

Imani waited with one arm crossed over her waist and a foot tapping the carpet.

When he returned to the line, there were no more voices in the background. He had clearly gone to a room alone to speak to her.

"Do not threaten me, Imani."

"Threaten you? I wouldn't dream of it. You're the king, after all."

"That is correct."

"But as queen, I must have *some* power. Some free will of my own." She filled her voice with caustic ice.

"Not the will to walk away from our marriage. If you believe that, you've sorely miscalculated."

"Maybe you're the one who miscalculated." Imani allowed a healthy dose of humor to infuse her voice.

"Imani—"

"I hope you have a productive trip."

"*Imani!*"

She hung up the phone. It rang immediately but she ignored it and checked the time. She should meet Yasmin downstairs now.

She gathered up her notes and other items and drop them into a large handbag. She then turned off the phone, which hadn't stopped its incessant ringing since she hung up. She dropped it into the bag and then pulled a second phone out of one of the desk drawers. It wasn't fully charged, but she dropped it into the bag, as well.

Then she marched out of the office with a smile on her face.

20

Today had been long, but ended on a positive note. Imani now had a good idea of how the literacy program worked and how it aided the outlying communities. When they walked through the makeshift teaching centers set up outdoors or at someone's home, she met and spoke to dozens of women and girls who dropped in during the day to take classes. But like Yasmin, she wondered how to quantify the program's success to justify the doubling of the budget Yasmin wanted.

Both women climbed into the back of the SUV, and the driver headed out of the last of the communities they visited for the day. They both removed the shaylas they'd worn with their pantsuits out of respect for the conservative nature of the people in the countryside, and settled down for the ride back to Kabatra.

"You probably won't believe this, but the reason I also want to expand the program is because there are conservative members of the Parliament who think we're funneling too much of the government's money into free programs that provide little benefit to the country as a whole. I need to get

Wasim on my side, or the program could be shut down completely."

Imani couldn't believe her ears. "What? That's ridiculous. It's clearly beneficial."

"Clear to you and me, but I couldn't get one single member of Parliament to send a representative to come see how the program works. They simply don't care." Yasmin sighed. "I don't understand why they would have a problem with expanding programs that help people."

"We have similar problems with certain members of The Most High Council in Zamibia. They can always find money for their pet projects like expanding training facilities for the soldiers in their communities or paying for grander buildings and furniture for their administrative offices. But there's always a budgetary crisis whenever we need to fund programs for the less fortunate. Dahlia said the same problems exist in the United States. Extremists weaponize Christianity and use it against the poor, the less fortunate, and to limit women's rights and protections in favor of men. Like many people who want to keep power, they blame the less fortunate for their own plight and prefer to have an uneducated population because they're easier to control."

Yasmin shook her head in disgust. "I wish we could get rid of the whole lot of them."

They both laughed.

Yasmin's phone beeped when they left the dead zone where there was no cellular signal. She glanced down at the screen and frowned.

"What's wrong?" Imani asked.

"Farouk sent me a text. This Hilton deal is so stressful. It's his biggest one yet, and he's very worried. I have to do my wifely duty and convince him he can handle the project." She tapped out a message.

They had such a cute relationship. They stayed in close

contact with each other and were always holding hands or if they were seated together, Yasmin would rest her head on his shoulder. And it was clear how much Farouk adored his wife and respected her opinions. Her support and ideas were an integral part of their relationship.

Imani tamped down the bit of envy she experienced, disappointed that she was in a very different situation. There was no evidence that Wasim saw her as anything more than his wife and the future mother of his children. He didn't seek out her opinion and he hadn't once asked about any of her projects.

Yasmin completed the text and asked, "When does Wasim return?"

"Day after tomorrow."

"I remember when Farouk and I were newlyweds. Any time apart always seemed like forever. I know you'll be happy when Wasim is back."

Imani smiled but didn't respond.

Yasmin's phone beeped as Farouk answered her message. Her sister-in-law started texting again, and she stared out at the passing countryside, eyes traveling over the green hills, sheep, and horses grazing on the grass, wondering what Wasim was doing now.

Wasim lied.

He lied so he could exit a very important meeting, claimed an emergency and left two representatives behind because he couldn't concentrate after his conversation with Imani. He managed to get through most of the day, but toward the end, he made up an excuse and opted out of the evening meal and the next day's meetings.

As night fell, he stepped out of the elevator on the top floor of the palace and stormed through the halls looking for Imani.

When one of her maids approached, he glared at her. "Where is my wife?" he asked, tugging on his tie. He could hardly breathe. His suit, tie, and socks—every article of clothing on his body constricted him.

"She is not here, Your Excellency."

"Where. Is. She?" He'd called all three of her phones several times and she hadn't answered them once or returned any of his messages.

"She left this morning and hasn't been back—"

"Get her social secretary to my apartment *now*. I will be waiting."

"Yes, Your Excellency." The maid bowed her head and ran off.

Wasim followed the young woman out the door and stalked to his apartment. He tossed his jacket and tie on a chair in the living room and paced the floor.

She couldn't have left him, could she? Was she on a plane to Zamibia?

Traveling out of the country took a coordinated effort of bodyguards, airport clearance, and a whole host of organizing that she couldn't have done on short notice.

Or could she? Imani was resourceful.

A timid knock came on the door. "Yes?" he yelled.

His manservant opened the door. "Zariah is here to see you, Your Excellency."

"Send her in," Wasim said, waving his hand agitatedly.

Zariah entered, and his manservant hovered outside the open door.

Poise kept Zariah's spine straight, but fear pooled in her eyes.

"Can *you* tell me where my wife is?" he asked.

She held an electronic tablet in her hand and looked down at the screen. "A-according to the schedule, she had a meeting with Princess Yasmin this morning."

"Where is she now?" Wasim asked, the frayed edges of his patience about to snap if she didn't give him more information soon.

"I-I am not certain. There was nothing else on her schedule for today."

Wasim walked over to Zariah. She visibly shook as he approached.

"Am I not king?" he asked, uncaring that he sounded like an imperial jackass.

She frowned and swallowed, confusion in her face. "I-yes, Your Excellency. You are king."

"Then how is it that I am king and no one can tell me where my wife is? When I left this morning, she was here. Now she is not."

She swallowed again.

"Where is my wife, Zariah?"

"I-I don't know, Your Excellency," she whispered.

Wasim leaned closer. "Then *find her and bring her to me!*"

Zariah closed her eyes, looking like she was about to burst into tears.

His manservant stepped into the room. "Your Excellency, we will work on this right away." He bowed and without touching Zariah, guided the trembling woman back out the door.

THE MINUTE WASIM received word that Imani had arrived on the palace grounds, he went to her apartment. He turned one of her chairs toward the door, sat down, and waited.

She strolled into the bedroom like nothing was amiss and pulled up short when she saw him.

"Did Zariah tell you I wanted to see you?" he asked.

"Yes, but not only her. Seems you've been a complete ass to

everyone. I could barely take a step without one of the servants telling me that you wanted to see me."

"And yet you are here, in your apartment instead of mine. Like I knew you'd be."

"I've been gone all day, Wasim. I wanted to clean up first. I told your manservant I would come see you shortly. You would have gotten the message if you were over there instead of here." Her eyes challenged him with not a shred of remorse in their dark depths.

"Where have you been? I've been trying to reach you since I came back."

"With Yasmin. We went into the countryside. She wanted me to see the work she was doing to combat illiteracy among the women. When we came back to Kabatra, we went to dinner together. Is that all right with you?"

"You could have called. You could have returned one of the many messages I left on all of your cell phones."

"I haven't checked my phones. I turned off my personal phone this morning, left one in the office, and the third one died while I was out."

Wasim pushed to his feet. "I have been going out of my mind with worry. I even called your father." He'd felt like an idiot, hinting around, trying to find out if she was in Zamibia without actually asking.

Imani's eyes widened. "Why? I expected you back after tomorrow. Maybe you should've told me you planned to come back early. Then I could have been here patiently waiting for your return."

"Do you think this is a joke? Someone should always know where you are. Anything could have happened to you."

"Zariah knew where I was."

"Hardly."

She flung up her hands in exasperation. "I was with Yasmin. You're obviously very angry, and I don't know why. You couldn't reach me for a few hours, that's it. You're overreacting."

"You said you would leave me!" he thundered.

Imani's mouth fell open. "You really thought I went back to Zamibia?"

Wasim let out a heavy breath to calm down. His head throbbed. "Yes. Because you got what you wanted. The agreement has been signed."

She walked slowly toward one of the tables near the bed and set down her bag and scarf. "I know I said that, but I didn't mean it."

"You can't say such things to me, Imani. I couldn't concentrate on my work. All I could think about was getting back here to you."

He was opening himself up to her, baring his soul in a way that made him extremely uncomfortable. This knowledge would give her too much power, yet he couldn't stop talking.

"Next time I'll call." She turned to face him. So calm. So cool. As if this conversation bored her and the idea of him going out of his mind didn't matter.

"I want you."

Eyes widening, she took a step back. "Now?"

"Yes. Now."

He stalked over to her and thrust his fingers into her hair.

"I'm filthy," she whispered, even as he felt her body leaned into his.

"You are never filthy to me."

He tossed aside his shirt and roughly removed her clothes, fingers trembling with the power of his need, yet somehow managing to maintain enough control to not shred her garments in his haste to get her naked.

Placing her on the bed, he whispered, "This is not filthy." He dragged his tongue along the slit at the apex of her thighs and she cried out. "This is not filthy." He sucked her chocolate nipples and squeezed her breasts while rubbing his hands over the curves of her waist and hips.

He unzipped and then spread her legs, almost nutting as he looked down at her, glistening and swollen in her need for him. Briefly closing his eyes, he fisted his erection and guided himself into her body.

Imani opened, granting him access into the depths of her quivering flesh.

"This is how I want you to greet me when I come home. With your legs open and your body ready," he whispered gutturally.

He sank into her, almost collapsing but then recharged with deep, forceful strokes that pushed air from his lungs and prompted breathless cries from her lips.

He started slow but increased the tempo as her moans filled his ears. His hard chest crushed her breasts and silently, he prayed for the stamina to hold back until she climaxed, but it was so damn hard to maintain control when she writhed and moaned with every thrust.

The past twelve hours had been a nightmare. The thought of her not being here when he came back had consumed and tortured him beyond anything he'd ever experienced before.

As she came, her cries fueled his faster, deeper thrusts. She gripped the sheets and her body quivered around him, while his breaths came out as heavy huffs near her ear.

"I will never grow tired of the sight of you coming for me. *Only* me," Wasim groaned, and let go with a final thrust and squeeze of her ass as he emptied inside of her. He kept the full weight of his body off her by resting on his arms. His head fell to the scented curve of her neck, his labored breaths pounding against her collarbone.

"Never leave me," he whispered hoarsely.

The words tumbled from his lips in a shameless plea. Not like the voice of a king, the ruler of all he could see, whose every sentence became law as soon as they were uttered from his lips. With her, he was merely a man, desperate to hold onto the most valuable person in his life. The one person he was beginning to think his heart couldn't beat without.

"I didn't think you cared." Imani quickly turned her face away as if embarrassed she'd spoken the words.

Wasim lifted his head. "Why would you say that? Look at me." He twisted her face back around to him. "Why would you say that?"

"Because this is all I am to you. A body to lose yourself in." Hurt filled her eyes, and she pushed him off and rolled away. "It's time for you to go back to your apartment, isn't it?" Her voice was completely devoid of emotion.

Wasim froze in shock. Then he fell onto his back and stared up at the chandelier. The glaring light had shined down on them the entire time they made love. He considered not moving, but then thought better of it. He had too much to think about.

"I'm leaving, but we will talk tomorrow."

She didn't reply.

Wasim eased from the bed, got dressed, and left her alone.

21

T he next morning, Wasim rose early. He hadn't slept much anyway because Imani stayed on his mind. He ate breakfast and then went down to the administrative offices to work. The rooms were mostly silent, as much of the staff hadn't arrived yet.

The IT guy bowed briefly at him as they passed in the hallway before Wasim entered his office. He sank into the chair behind his enormous desk and rubbed his bearded jaw.

Women never failed to confuse him. He thought he had done the right thing by showing Imani that he signed the blasted agreement. He assumed she'd be pleased he sent her proof and that might ease the tension that hovered like a specter over their marriage. He was certain the unsigned agreement remained a barrier between them, why she'd been withdrawn and cool except for the hot nights they spent between the sheets.

Though she did express thanks, she'd been anything but thankful. There had been no joy or appreciation in her voice. Only censure and ire.

He'd been so busy since his father's death, tackling the

daunting task of the issues at the palace. Much of his time in recent weeks had been spent reorganizing his Cabinet, and he'd removed a third of the advisors, which caused a minor uproar. He filled his time with these tasks, giving her space he thought would ease her into their marital relationship and her role as queen. Wrong again. Her comments after they had made love last night showed his thought process had been flawed. She actually wanted to spend time with him and was hurt that he'd limited the amount of time he spent with her.

Aih, he had a lot to learn.

When Talibah arrived, he told her to cancel all his plans for the following day and have Imani's secretary do the same for her schedule. When she expressed surprise, he explained he was going to spend the day with his wife.

At her pleased expression, he gleaned that was absolutely the right answer and set out to wrap up as much as he could by day's end.

"WHERE ARE WE GOING?" Imani asked.

She and Wasim rode in the back of the limo, and all she knew was that they were going to the beach for a picnic. Nothing else about the day's activities had been shared with her, and though she knew much of Barrakesch, she wasn't familiar with the road they were on.

"Have I ever told you about Muriah Beach?" Wasim looked relaxed in his typical uniform of a white shirt and black slacks. The shirt was unbuttoned at the collar, and the shirtsleeves rolled up at the arms gave a tantalizing peek at wiry forearms sprinkled with fine hairs.

"No," Imani replied, but the name was vaguely familiar.

"It's a private beach accessible only to the royal family. We're going to spend the day there. There is a small house there we can use, but we'll be entirely alone—well, except for our security, the chef, his assistants, and our help. I sent the chef and the others ahead yesterday to prepare the place for us."

A small thrill of pleasure sparked inside of Imani. They were going to spend the whole day together. It shouldn't matter so much, but it did.

When they arrived at their destination, the royal couple entered the so-called small house, which was actually a sprawling beach house with ten bedrooms, eleven baths, and an indoor pool.

In the great room, decorated in patterned chairs that seemed comfortable and cozy, Imani looked out at the water. Outside on the balcony, contemporary wicker chairs with teal cushions were grouped together around tables with unlit votive candles on top. Beyond that, she saw a stone pathway that led down a gentle incline, shadowed by shrubs and palm trees to the clear blue of the Gulf lapping at the shore.

"It's beautiful," she breathed as she took in the scenic view.

"I thought you would like it," Wasim said, right behind her.

She clasped her hands and turned to face him. "What are we going to do first?"

"How about horseback riding to start?"

A playful smile lifted the right corner of his mouth. He hadn't smiled much recently, and the transformation in his face reminded her of the fun they used to have, before the bitterness that developed between them.

"Are you talking about a race?" Imani asked.

"You're not ready for a race," Wasim said dismissively.

"Oh, really?" She pretended to be affronted. "Maybe you're not ready to lose."

With his hands behind his back, he took two steps closer and her skin heated at his nearness. Gazing up at him, she became lost for a moment in his copper-brown eyes. Were all women this enamored with their spouses? He never failed to arouse her passions and make her heart beat with much too much speed beneath her breast.

"May the best horseman win," Wasim said in his velvety voice.

"You mean, may the best horse*woman*."

"When will you learn?" He laughed softly and shook his head, which only made Imani more determined to beat him and knock the cocky smirk off his face.

They changed into more comfortable clothes while the help prepared their horses for the ride. Instead of saddles, they both chose colorful padded seats that draped over the horses' ribs. Imani climbed onto a brown and white stallion, while Wasim lifted onto a black mare.

They started out at a slow pace along the water's edge. The horses stepped into the rolling waves, the white crests lapping at their legs as they trotted through the water. Wasim pointed out dolphins leaping in the distance, only one of the many marine animals that filled Barrakesch's deep waters. There were hundreds of varieties of fish and sharks much further out.

When Imani and Wasim reached the end of the beach, they both turned around to head back the way they'd come, and when their eyes met, a silent challenge was issued. Imani took off on the stallion and Wasim shot after her right away.

The horses' hooves sank into the wet sand along the water's edge, and Imani crouched over the powerful beast and urged him to go faster, but she was no match for Wasim and his mare. He passed by and then glanced back at her. The breeze coming off the Gulf whipped his black hair into frenzied disarray, his white clothing billowed around his arms and legs, while laughing eyes softened his features. For a moment, she didn't care if she won or lost. She simply wanted to look at him and bask in the positive energy pouring out of him.

Still, she had a race to win, but Wasim showed her no

mercy. He led the way to the original spot and handed her a big loss.

He jumped lightly to the ground onto his bare feet, and Imani, laughing and panting, looked down at him. "You have an unfair advantage."

"How so?" he asked.

"Because you ride all the time," she said.

With his hands at her waist, he helped her down, and she landed between him and the horse. Wasim brushed her hair back from her face that the wind had mercilessly whipped about, and her skin tingled where he touched.

Bending his head to her ear, he said, "Yet you challenged me. You should learn to pick your battles."

Her heart raced at his closeness and the whisper of his breath against her earlobe. "And you should learn to show mercy."

"Did you want me to let you win?" he asked, lifting an eyebrow.

"I'm suggesting you could have shown a little mercy, that's all."

"I'll show you mercy when we go for a swim. I promise not to drown you."

"As if you could. I was practically born in the ocean."

"And you were also the better horse*woman*. We'll see soon enough what kind of swimming skills you have, won't we?"

"Yes, we will." Imani walked ahead of him and then glanced over her shoulder. Feeling playful, she said, "Race you!" Then she took off running.

"Hey!" Wasim scrambled up the incline after her.

THE CHEF and his helpers had a spread of fruit and citrus-flavored water waiting for them. They indulged in the refreshments and then gathered their belongings to enjoy the rest of their time on the beach.

Helpers set up umbrellas and chairs and a table on the sand, and when Imani got ready to disrobe, Wasim dismissed the male bodyguards so they were alone.

She removed the opaque cover she'd worn down to the beach and unveiled an electric blue halter top bikini. She even put a little extra wiggle in her body as she removed her clothes, knowing Wasim's eyes were on her. When she turned to him with the sunblock in her hands, his eyes were clouded with lust.

"Could you do my back, please?" she asked.

He took the bottle without a word, and she let him rub the cream into her shoulders and back. Then he lowered to his haunches and got her legs, too. The touch of his hand should have been nonsexual, but she couldn't help getting a little turned on. By the time he finished massaging the lotion into her inner thighs and the underside of her ass—which received much more attention than was necessary—her nipples had beaded against the bikini top and she was a little breathless.

He finished the job by covering her arms, chest, and belly, his warm hand sliding over her heated skin with a slow, silky touch. When he finally let her go she felt deprived and wished he'd continue touching her.

She returned the favor by rubbing the lotion over his muscular back and down along his hard thighs and calves— taking her time to appreciate the beauty of sinew and muscle covered in golden skin. She was just as thorough as he was and rubbed the lotion into his chest and abs with a lazy, circular motion that caused him to draw the occasional sharp breath. When she finished the task, Wasim tossed the bottle aside, dragged her close by the back of her neck, and plundered her mouth in a searing kiss.

When he released her, his shallow breaths feathered across her parted lips. "Ready to go into the water?" he asked.

While the look in his eyes said he wanted to do anything but go into the water, she appreciated that he was sticking to their planned schedule.

"I would love to."

Wasim took her hand and they walked to the water. They splashed around, jumped into the waves, and floated on their backs as they let the sun's rays toast their skin into a darker hue. Their playfulness included Imani jumping on his back or Wasim tossing her into the waves.

Worry-free, Imani lost track of how much time they spent out there. Every time they grew tired, they went back to the shore, relaxed on the chairs, and rehydrated. Then they went back into the water for more swimming, splashing, and playing.

Her grumbling stomach caused Imani to say, "I'm ready to eat now."

"I am, too, actually," Wasim admitted.

They went back to the shore where they both covered up and Wasim called for their lunch.

Two female servants delivered a picnic basket filled with a choice of sandwiches, more fresh fruit, figs with creamy goat cheese, and more of the refreshing citrus water.

After they ate, their full bellies kept them relaxing on the chairs. Wasim reclined in his lounger and looked at her.

"What?" Imani said.

"Come here."

"Why?"

"Come. Here."

She wanted to be stubborn. To refuse him, but her feet moved of their own volition and took her across the small divide. She rested her knee on the edge of his chair, and he took her hand with the platinum and diamond wedding band.

"When I tell you to do something, you should do it."

"I'm not afraid of you."

"You should be. My word is law. I am the ultimate authority in Barrakesch."

"And you do want an obedient wife. How sad for you that's not what you ended up with."

"Are you sure, *habibti*?"

She tried to yank away her hand, but he tightened his hold and chuckling, pulled her down on top of him. As Imani relaxed and closed her eyes, Wasim smoothed a hand under the coverup and cupped her bottom. He squeezed her ass several times and she moaned, settling more comfortably on top of him before he patted her left cheek and left his hand there.

That was the last thing she remembered—his hand resting possessively on her bottom as she lay on top of him—before she dozed off.

She woke up when Wasim shook her awake. Groggily, she opened her eyes and saw the sun had already set.

"It's time to go back to the house," he said quietly.

"Okay," Imani said, glancing up at the darkening sky.

He gave her a tender kiss, holding his mouth against hers for long time before he finally released her.

They slowly made their way back to the house, with her tucked into his side and an arm around his waist. After spending the day together playing, laughing, and even sleeping, being this close to him felt extremely natural.

While the helpers went down to the beach to gather up the items they'd left, she and Wasim took showers in separate bathrooms and changed clothes before the last part of the day commenced.

22

Their meal consisted of grilled trout, sautéed vegetables, and *bissap*, a popular Zamibian drink made from dried hibiscus flowers. They ate out on the balcony with only a few lights on, and votive candles flickering on the table. The sound of the Arabian Sea rolling forward across the sands over and over again was their background music.

As the meal came to an end, Imani dabbed her lips with the white napkin. "That was absolutely delicious."

"Yes, it was," Wasim agreed.

His eyes lingered on her face and made her feel a little shy. Her cheeks warmed and she cast her eyes down at her lap.

"We haven't laughed and talked to each other like this in a while," he said quietly.

"No, we haven't."

"I miss our friendship."

"I miss it, too," Imani admitted.

The chef, a tall heavy-set man with a thick mustache and beard, came out with one of the helpers behind him. "Will there be anything else, Your Excellency, Your Royal Highness? Dessert?"

Wasim looked at Imani, deferring to her, but she shook her head.

"Coffee, tea?" the chef asked, looking from one to the other. Imani shook her head again.

"Nothing for me. Everything was delicious," Wasim said. He waved a hand at the table and indicated they should clear away the dishes.

They did just that and disappeared inside.

They were alone for several minutes before Wasim asked, "Do you want to walk away from this marriage?"

She lowered her gaze. Walking away was the last thing on her mind, especially after today. Today gave her hope that they could have a normal relationship. Like him, she'd missed their camaraderie.

Wasim scraped back his chair and extended a hand to her. She took it and they walked to the grouping of wicker chairs with teal cushions. Wasim sat down first so that he was facing the sea and pulled her down against him.

"We need to talk," he said. "I'm not very good at talking, but I can listen if there's anything you want to say."

Wrapped in his arms and not having to look at him, Imani felt comfortable enough to open up.

"I don't want to walk away from our marriage." She heard him breathe what could only be described as a sigh of relief. His hand stroked comfortingly over her hair. "But since we've been married, I feel like I'm little more than a body for you."

"I can see how you would think that. I suppose it's because ever since we kissed in Estoria, I've been consumed with thoughts of you. I've been consumed with thoughts of you ever since you stepped off the plane to attend graduate school in Barrakesch and Kofi told me to keep an eye on you. I should be angry at him for doing that because his request forced me to keep my distance. But Estoria changed everything, and there have been times when I wished I could cut off my hands so I wouldn't feel the need to reach for you."

Imani twisted so that she could see his face. "Wasim..." She touched a finger to his cheek.

He took her hand and kissed her palm.

Imani sighed. "I've been angry at you, and I want to explain. Obviously, I wasn't happy about the way we got married, and then the only use you seemed to have for me was sex. We never talk about issues anymore or problems that we could solve together. You don't share your work with me, and I don't feel like I can share mine with you. Before I felt like we were equals, but now..." She shook her head as words failed her.

"You've always been so capable, I didn't think you needed me to say or do anything to encourage you. You've always impressed me, Imani. Surely you know that."

"I suppose." She shrugged to downplay her need for his respect. "I know it's unfair, but I worry that you'll treat me the way my father has all my life."

"Do you feel I've hindered you in any way?"

"No," she admitted.

"I respect you. You are an amazing woman, and I am lucky to have you ruling by my side. Both of our countries are lucky to have you and your brilliant mind and caring heart."

"Thank you."

"*But*," Wasim added, holding her attention with direct eye contact, "There is one thing you must understand. While I respect you and would never try to stifle you because I want you to thrive, you are my wife, and it's my responsibility to take care of you. I take my responsibilities very seriously. Are we clear on that?"

"Yes. I suppose being married to a king means I'll want for nothing?"

"Not one single thing." He pulled her on top of him so that she straddled his thighs. "Anything else?"

"Nothing I can think of...for now."

"So...does the sex and the respect have to be mutually exclusive?"

She laughed. "Wasim..."

"I'm asking because I need to know how far I can push tonight." He smoothed a hand under her abaya.

Imani cast a glance inside the house, but the great room was empty. The servants were all gone.

Wasim slapped her right butt cheek.

She flinched—not from pain, but from the delicious pleasure of the blow. "Are you asking if we're on the sex part of the evening now that the conversation is over?"

"Yes."

"Yes, we're on the sex part of the evening," Imani said softly.

With a wicked grin, Wasim stood with her in his arms, and she wound her legs around his waist. He walked with her back to the master bedroom and brought them both to a shuddering climax.

WASIM REENTERED the bedroom with a bottle of water. He handed the balance to Imani and she finished it off. He set the empty bottle on the side table, and she cuddled up next to him on the bed.

"I never got to tell you about my conversation with your sister," she said, looping an arm across his chest.

Wasim rested against the pillows with one arm folded behind his head. "Tell me about it."

She caught him up on her visit with Yasmin and what they observed with the women and girls. "The only problem is, she needs to get that money, and that's where you come in. She needs you to get Parliament to include the additional funds in the budget so you can sign off on it."

"She should be convincing them to do it, not asking me to do it."

"But how do we convince them? Yasmin can't get a single member to send a representative to talk to the women about how much they enjoy the program. Could you make them do it?" she asked tentatively. She really wanted the program to get funded to the levels Yasmin needed.

Wasim chuckled softly. "I could, but that would cause resentment and other problems down the line. I'm already in Parliament's crosshairs, and I have to pick my battles. And though I could dissolve the entire group and start from scratch —like a certain Zambian woman pointed out—that is the drastic, nuclear option. I think the best way to convince Parliament to invest more in the program is to let the women tell them in their own words what the literacy initiative means to them."

"How? In a report they probably won't read?"

Wasim was silent for a moment. Then he said, "Through commercials."

"Commercials?" Imani raised up on one elbow.

"Yes. Film the women and the girls, and air the commercials on television. Let them tell the whole country how much the program helps them by giving examples. Then present the needs of the budget. Not every member will be swayed, but it's a good way to pressure the dissenting members of the body to get them to do the right thing, without actually pressuring them."

"That's sneaky."

"Sometimes you have to be sneaky."

"Okay, but I don't know if Yasmin has money to do commercials. I have to check with her."

"If she doesn't, we'll find the money from somewhere.

There are multiple miscellaneous accounts, or we could shift the money from another program. We'll figure it out." His eyes were indulgent as he smoothed a strand of hair back from her face.

"Thank you," Imani said.

"I'm not doing you a favor. It's the right thing to do." He studied her face. "You have something to say?"

Imani wanted to sort through the words before she spoke. Finally, she said, "I have a very odd relationship with my father. He loves me, but he treats me like I don't matter. Like my ideas are silly—noble, but silly. And why would a woman have to worry about independence when she can have a man take care of her?"

"And you don't want a man to take care of you?"

"I can take care of myself, and it's nice to be seen as an equal. But it's nice to have a supportive hand."

"Never worry about that. You will always have my support."

Satisfied, Imani rested her head atop his shoulder, happier than she had been in a very long time.

23

Imani felt the mattress depress as Wasim climbed in behind her. He had already stripped down to his boxers. His bare arms and chest enveloped her in warm, golden skin.

"You never sleep in your apartment anymore," she murmured, tucking her bottom into the vee created by his hips and legs.

He slid a knee between hers. "I like it better in here. Everything is soft and smells so good." He caressed her breasts under the silk nightie and nipped her neck.

Imani laughed softly. "I'm glad you like what you find in here."

Most nights over the past few weeks, Wasim had slept in her bedroom. The only times he hadn't was when he worked late and didn't want to disturb her when he came in.

Over the past couple of days, they'd played host to the President of the United States and her husband. A formal dinner had taken place the first night and another one this evening, which wrapped up later than expected. Imani and the president's husband had retired to bed, leaving Wasim and the president to continue their conversation. She hadn't expected him to come to her tonight, but she was pleased that he'd broken away early enough to join her in bed.

"The only event on the agenda tomorrow is the breakfast, correct?" Imani asked, yawning.

"Yes, then another photo op, and then the president meets with other officials before she flies out in the afternoon."

They were quiet for a few minutes and then Imani said, "I saw Yasmin singing to her baby today. She has such a beautiful voice." Yasmin was now almost seven months pregnant.

"My mother used to sing to us all the time," Wasim said quietly.

It was so rare that Imani heard him talk about his mother, her eyes popped open and she went still, waiting for more information. When he didn't continue, she said, "Tell me more about her."

He resettled at her back and when he spoke, she heard the smile in his voice. "She was happy all the time. She used to chase Yasmin and I around the palace and played with us and kissed us often. I can't remember her ever raising her voice at me. She might get annoyed or wag a finger, but she always remained so...sweet."

Imani smiled. "I take it she wasn't the disciplinarian."

"No. That role belonged to my father. My mother soothed our fears, kissed our bruises, and comforted us when we were sad."

"How did she die?"

"She drowned."

"I know that, but how?" Imani asked gently. She played with the tip of one of his fingers.

"On one of my family's yachts in the Mediterranean. She and my father had decided to slip away for some private time without me and Yasmin for a change. My mother left first, and he planned to meet her later because he had to take care of some business. The night he was to arrive, somehow she fell over into the water. None of the staff knew it happened, and she couldn't swim."

Imani chest tightened as she listened.

"Not one person knew she was missing. Can you believe that? A yacht with over a hundred crew members, and not one damn person knew she was gone until my father's helicopter landed that night and they couldn't find her." Rage simmered in his voice. "He was devastated. We were devastated. When he returned, he fired everyone on that boat."

"I'm so sorry, but thank you for sharing that with me," Imani whispered. She clutched his hand to her chest.

"That's what I want for my children. A woman who clearly loves kids."

"I love kids," Imani said.

He pulled her closer. "Then lucky for you, you'll be the mother of my children."

"Lucky for me, huh?"

"Mhmm. Are you still going to Zamibia in a few weeks?" He threaded their fingers together.

"Yes. They've finalized some of the staff and managers for the oil rig, and I want to check out the office they have set up in the village on the coast."

"That sounds like a good idea. I'm sure you'll whip them into shape if the work isn't up to standard," Wasim murmured, sounding sleepy.

"I'll do my best." Imani smiled and snuggled deeper into his arms.

WASIM SAT cross-legged on the floor at the traditional Barrakeschi restaurant with Farouk and Akmal. It was Saturday night, and Akmal had rented out the entire restaurant and called the impromptu meeting because he complained that the three of them hadn't spent any time together in a while.

Farouk had finally closed the Hilton deal, so celebrating was an additional good reason for them to get together. So far, their conversation had been the usual as they caught up in each other's lives.

But out of the blue, Akmal said, "The old men are still not pleased that you married Imani."

Wasim briefly eyed his brother across the table, and it dawned on him that this was the real reason he'd wanted to get together.

He knew about the concerns of the conservative faction of the Parliament. He'd heard the whispers from the beginning, that he was marrying an "outsider," a coded word that meant Imani wasn't Muslim. For those members, his decision to marry her was another example of his progressive ways, but they knew better than to make those comments to his face.

He'd never told Imani about the negative rumblings, but he wouldn't be surprised if she was aware of their displeasure. Only because King Khalid had approved of their marriage before his death had the entire process gone so well and there hadn't been any protests.

And what could they do now anyway? She and he were married, and she was part of this family.

He picked up a circle of grilled eggplant with a dollop of *labneh* and olive oil on it. "The old men will soon be dead and replaced by younger men. Their opinions matter very little to me."

"You're not concerned at all?" Farouk asked.

"Why should I be? We're married, and there's nothing anyone outside of the two of us can do to change that."

A look passed between both men.

"What does that look mean?" Wasim asked immediately.

Akmal smirked. "Are you in love with your wife?" He said the words as if they were an accusation.

Imani had seen marriage as a lifelong commitment to the person you love. Not a lifelong commitment to the person you *might* fall in love with, and their differing views had certainly presented a challenge.

But Wasim had only recently come to admit his love for her, to himself. He hadn't said a word to anyone else, and certainly not to her, yet. Their affection for each other had blossomed and grown, but that didn't mean these intense emotions he now experienced were reciprocated.

He could even admit that getting her to marry him was more self-serving than he originally acknowledged. When he'd lost his father, he'd used that as an excuse to hold onto her. To hold onto her laughter, her unmatched beauty, and adventurous spirit. He'd needed her and losing her had presented itself as an obstacle to be overcome by any means necessary.

"And if I am?" he asked.

"I think it's wonderful," Akmal said. "Oh, how the mighty have fallen."

"Spoken like a man who would do anything for his wife," Farouk added.

"And I would," Wasim confirmed.

"How does she feel about you?"

He decided to be honest. "That, I don't know, but I think she's getting there. We're happy, at least."

"Well, look at us. Three happily married men. We should drink to that." Akmal held up his Coke and Wasim and Farouk touched their glasses against his. "To our wives."

"To our lives," Farouk and Wasim repeated.

Then all three men laughed.

24

W asim finished dictating a letter and then deposited the file into the drive for Talibah to retrieve later. As he clicked out of the program, the phone on his desk rang.

"Her Royal Highness Queen Imani is on her way back to the palace and should be here in a few minutes."

"Thank you. I'll wrap up and meet her upstairs."

"Yes, Your Excellency."

He hung up and quickly reviewed a few more files. He'd promised Imani to take a break and have dinner with her tonight. Tomorrow night he had an administrative meeting that would certainly last through dinner, and she left for Zamibia the next day.

He logged off the computer and then exited the office. "Go home, Talibah," he said on the way out.

His assistant smiled and nodded, but he guessed if he came back down later, she'd still be at her desk.

He took the elevator to the sixth floor, where Imani met him in the large, open entrance wearing a purple abaya with white and lavender detailing on the sleeves, her hair loose and curling in a sexy way beside her cheeks, and a smile on her face.

"How was your day?" She tipped up her head, and he dropped a kiss to her puckered lips.

"Long, busy." Better now that he saw her.

They seldom saw each other during the day because of their busy schedules filled with meetings and various tasks. Imani also traveled outside of the palace more often than he did. Because of her charitable work and the organizations she supported, she had to remain visible and took lots of photographs because her image was needed to generate publicity.

One of the projects, the Women & Girls Literacy Initiative she had worked on with Yasmin, received the additional funding it needed after they followed his advice and ran a well-thought-out advertising campaign on television and extended their efforts to billboards across the cities and in the countryside.

He'd become better attuned to her moods, as well. He distinctly remembered a conversation they'd had only last week.

Imani's name popped up on the LCD screen of Wasim's personal phone.

"Hello? Is everything okay?" he asked. It was unusual for her to call him at work in the middle of the day.

"Yes, yes, I just..."

"You just what...?" Wasim asked.

"Nothing. I'm not even sure why I called." She let out an embarrassed laugh. "I'll let you get back to work."

"Imani."

"Yes?"

He quickly glanced at his open calendar on the computer. "Have lunch with me today. We'll go to that Indian restaurant in the old

part of town. The one you like and claim you introduced me to, but I
seriously doubt."

"I did introduce you to it."

"If you say so. Are you free?"

"Are you sure you're not too busy?" she asked, her voice full of
hesitation.

"I'm not too busy for you."

"If we go, we'll have to make arrangements now so security can
sweep the area before we arrive."

"I'll take care of that."

"Okay. Twelve o'clock?" Her voice became more upbeat.

"Twelve-thirty works better. Meet me downstairs at that time."

"Okay. I'll see you then."

"How was your day?" Wasim asked.

"Interesting," Imani said with a little smile on her face, like
she had a secret.

"Oh?" Wasim trailed her out to the balcony where a feast
had already been set. Jugs of juice and covered dishes filled the
table, stoking his appetite.

It was nice to have someone else take care of the details,
look out for his well-being, and in general, welcome him home.

He now understood why his father had never fully recovered after his mother's sudden death. When you love someone
the way he had loved her, how could you possibly recover if you
lost them? They weren't only a part of your life, they were part
of *you*. You could never be whole again when part of you was
missing. And all the little things, the details, took on a more
profound meaning.

"Have a seat," Imani said, pointing to the chair at the head
of the table.

"What are you up to?" Wasim asked as he sat down.

"You'll see." Imani sat down across his thighs with the
secretive smile still on her face. "At first I was worried about

what I have to tell you, but then I thought, why worry? We're in a good place, right?"

"Of course. We have been for a while, and better than I expected." He was now very curious to hear what she had to say.

Imani nodded. "Good." She took a deep breath and then lifted the dome off one of the dishes. Instead of meat or rice or potatoes, there was an envelope inside.

Wasim frowned, watching as she removed it and took out a grainy photo. His mouth fell open.

All smiles, Imani beamed at him with glowing dark eyes.

"Is this what I think it is?" he asked in awe.

Imani nodded, her smile widening. "We're going to have a baby in seven months."

She barely got the words out before he clutched her face in his hands and gave her a sound kiss, devouring her lips as his heart filled with joy. When he finally released her, Imani laughed and bit her bottom lip.

"I guess you're happy?"

"I couldn't be happier. I..." Wasim was so overcome that for a moment he could barely speak. They were going to be parents. He rested his forehead against hers. "Imani...*habibti, hayati, rohi.*" She was the most important person in his life.

"Wasim," she whispered, voice trembling, tears shimmering in her eyes.

He cradled her face in his hands. "You are my everything, and now you wish to give me even more. I love you."

For so long he'd held in the words, knowing that his strong feelings for her might not be reciprocated because she'd told him that day when she finally agreed to marry him that she'd never love him. Those words echoed in his head at the most inopportune times, casting doubt in the middle of their happy union. But those words had been said in anger, and he believed her feelings had changed. Looking at her excitement at the prospect of them having a child together, he knew they had.

"*Moni fey-eh*," she whispered back in Mbutu, her tribal tongue. She had told him that she loved him, too.

They indulged in a slow, sensual kiss and then she sighed and rested her head on his shoulder.

"Do you still have to leave?" he asked.

"I'm afraid so. The plans have been made, but I won't be gone long. Less than a week."

"A lifetime." Wasim placed a hand on her flat belly and imagined the life growing there.

"I'll miss you, too. It'll be the longest time we've been apart since our ceremony. But I'll be back before you know it."

25

I *miss you already.*

Imani sent the text to Wasim and sank her teeth into her bottom lip as she waited for his response. She didn't have long to wait. Only a few minutes later, he texted back: *Don't make me come get you.*

She let out a soft laugh and sent a quick *I love you* text. He texted back the same, and then she slipped the phone into her bag.

Crossing her arms over her chest, she gazed out at the passing scenery of golden sand interrupted by tufts of green foliage on the long road from Kabatra to the private airport where the royal plane awaited her arrival.

Saying *I love you* came much easier than she had expected and would become easier still in the coming weeks as they grew more and more comfortable with each other. She thought back to how their marriage had initially started and marveled at how far they had come as a couple. Wasim had been right all along. Love could come after. Or in their case, had it been there all along? She'd certainly had feelings for him, and based on their conversations, he'd always had feelings for her.

The limo slowed to a crawl, and Imani turned her attention to the scene playing out in front of them. The SUV carrying four members of her security detail slowed to a stop to let an old farmer with stooped shoulders lead his sheep across the roadway. Not an unusual site in this part of the country, and they had left early enough that time was on their side.

The driver, an older man with deep wrinkles carved into his face that made him look older than he was, met her eyes in the rearview mirror. "Not too much longer, Your Highness."

Imani waved away any concern that she might be annoyed. "We have plenty of time, and he's simply doing his job."

She let her mind wander to the upcoming trip. She couldn't wait to tell her parents, especially her mother, that she was pregnant. Benu would be excited about becoming a grandmother and would no doubt start planning some type of celebratory event to commemorate her pregnancy at a later date, after she'd been pregnant for a few months.

Movement from the corner of her eye caused Imani to turn her head to the left, but what she saw caused alarm to spring to life in her stomach. A group of six men approached swiftly on horseback, all of them wearing traditional clothes and riding as if the hounds of hell pursued them. She straightened in the seat and stared. They all wore their *ghutras* pinned across the bridge of their noses, hiding their features so only their eyes were visible.

What was happening?

The power locks on the limo engaged, and her gaze lifted to the rearview mirror again where they met the driver's worried gaze. Without saying a word, his eyes darted to the right, and she saw five more men on horseback coming toward them from that direction.

The driver flung the vehicle into reverse and slammed into the SUV behind them filled with additional security. Imani gripped the seat and let out a soft cry at the impact. Her driver uttered a curse and quick, "I'm so sorry, Your Highness."

Then, shots rang out. Imani screamed and covered her ears.

The next series of events happened quickly. The limo sank toward the right as the tires were blown out. The same happened to the vehicle in front of them, and she was certain behind them as well, though she didn't turn around to look. The cars were incapacitated and they couldn't get away.

The bodyguards in the front vehicle hopped out, two on each side to combat the incoming men who'd gotten much closer in a matter of seconds. They fired off a series of shots, but instead of the men on horseback ending up with casualties, she watched in horror as three members of her security team collapsed to the roadway, clutching their necks as if someone had stabbed them with a knife.

More shots rang out in the front and behind the limo, and one of the men to the left tumbled from his horse. The lone remaining bodyguard scrambled to reload his weapon, and Imani's eyes widened as the men on horseback pulled their animals to a stop and hopped down almost simultaneously.

Unexpectedly, the old farmer ran up the front hood of the SUV and stood on top of the roof. The old farmer wasn't old after all. He moved with the speed and agility of a much younger man. He looked down at the guard, who shrunk against the outside of the vehicle, head twisting left to right as he took in the men who'd surrounded him. The farmer blew into a bamboo tube and the fourth bodyguard fell to the asphalt.

Using bamboo darts was a fighting tactic the Barrakeschis had borrowed from Zamibia during their long history of friendship. The poison came from a mollusk indigenous to Zamibia. Hunters had used the poison to take down wild game, but her tribe, the Mbutu, turned it into a weapon of war. The poison worked best when sent through the neck and quickly incapacitated its victim for several hours. The weapon was basic but effective and demonstrated these men didn't want to seriously hurt anyone.

At least, that's what she hoped. Because when she turned around, the same fate had befallen the guards in the SUV behind her. The men on horseback completely caged her and the driver in the limo. Hardly daring to breathe she was so frightened, Imani gripped the leather seat with both hands. Then she remembered her phone.

The farmer hopped off the top of the SUV and came walking slowly toward the limo. He definitely was young. She could see it in his eyes though she couldn't see his whole face. He yelled something to one of the men to his left, and the man came forward and pointed a rifle at the right passenger window at the front.

Standing back to avoid ricocheting bullets, he fired off a shot, but the bulletproof glass didn't break. Imani took the phone from her purse, and with trembling fingers hit redial to get Wasim. He was the last call she'd made that day. Unfortunately, she would not be reaching him now. Somehow, the men on horseback must have jammed the phones because she didn't have a signal. There was no way she was going to make any kind of call—to Wasim, emergency, or otherwise.

Another shot went off, and she jumped. They were going to keep shooting in the same spot to weaken the window. It would only be a matter of time before they got in.

The driver reached for the glove compartment.

"No!" He was going for a gun but they would kill him if he pulled it out.

"Your Highness..."

She winced as another shot hit the glass. "Don't. They'll kill you. And I don't think they want to kill anyone. They want me."

Another shot. And another. Each loud bang brought them

closer to getting inside and tightened the noose of fear that wound around her throat.

The glass didn't break, but it absorbed the blows and splintered into a spiderweb-like pattern. When it was sufficiently damaged, the farmer came forward and held up a ball-peen hammer that appeared to have a piece of ceramic attached to it. He whacked the window several times and the glass broke into small pieces.

He reached in and opened the door, and blew the poison dart at the neck of the driver, who quickly collapsed against the seat. Then he turned cool, emotionless eyes to Imani. He climbed across the driver and unlocked the back doors. They were immediately swung open by men on either side.

"Get out," one of the men said gruffly.

Before she could even think about responding, he caught her by the hand and dragged her from the vehicle. She let out a small yelp as she tumbled from the car.

"Be careful!" one of the men said, shoving the one who'd grabbed her.

The man's grip on her upper arm tightened as she straightened. She swung her eyes from left to right. She was out here all alone, surrounded and without any assistance. Where were they taking her? What were they going to do with her? She had to get away.

Quickly, instinctively, she swung her fist at the man holding her arm. The blow landed to the side of his face, and he howled in surprise and pain and quickly stepped back. Someone else came up behind her and she elbowed him and swung her fist into his nose. He hollered and stumbled back.

"Let me go!" she yelled.

She clenched her fingers and muscle memory shifted her body into a fighting stance with both fists held at chin level. She wasn't going down without a fight.

Quickly sizing up the men, she deduced they couldn't be

mercenaries or fighters. Their bodies were too relaxed because they assumed their size and number would be enough to intimidate her. They'd miscalculated.

She was scared but not intimidated. She was a fighter, a skill learned long ago thanks to the help of six brothers and Mbutu warrior blood running through her veins.

Yet even as she considered landing more blows, she noticed their hesitation. The way they looked from one to the other. They'd surrounded her but were afraid to hurt her. Not one of the punches she landed had received a retaliatory blow. They weren't going to fight back.

"I'm pregnant," she said, thinking that might help and they'd rethink this plan.

An awkward pause filled the air as they glanced quickly at each other and then turned their attention to the farmer, clearly the leader. None of them had expected this new development. They not only had the queen, they had her unborn child, too. The potential heir to the throne.

Too late, she saw movement at the corner of her eye, and something stung the back of her neck.

Then...lights out.

asim would never forget where he was when he learned that Imani's caravan had been ambushed. He was seated on the sofa in his office, reviewing the specs for the metro rail line, the next major project to be completed now that the budget had been approved.

A forceful, rapid knock on his office door caused him to stare at it in shock that anyone would dare pound so hard.

"Yes?"

His head of security, Mohammed, rushed in. A giant of a man who was at least six inches taller than Wasim, he came in holding a phone. Then he told Wasim they had lost contact with Imani's team, and there was a man on the line who said that he had Imani and a demand.

Wasim could feel the blood drain from his face. He jumped up from the sofa and snatched away the phone. He hit the Mute button. "Who is this?" he demanded.

A mechanically distorted voice came on the line. "Never mind who I am. We have Her Royal Highness Queen Imani with us."

"You must be insane," Wasim said. To kidnap a member of the royal family was unheard of. The act was a crime punishable by death. Only a crazy person would commit such an offense.

The mechanical voice laughed. "I assure you, I am quite sane."

"How is she? Is my wife safe?" He gripped the phone as fear surged within him.

"Yes."

"Before you tell me what you want, I need to know that she's safe. Nothing moves forward until you confirm that."

"You don't make the rules!"

"And you get nothing until I know my wife is safe." He would not budge. He'd quickly read the situation and suspected that standing up to this reckless fool—whoever he was—would be the best way to handle this interaction.

There was a long pause. Wasim tensed, his gaze meeting Mohammed's.

Finally, a response. "As you wish, Your Excellency." The mechanical voice dripped with sarcasm and Wasim gritted this teeth. He couldn't wait to put his hands around this man's throat.

A few seconds later, a video came through on the phone while Wasim and Mohammed watched. Imani wore the same clothes she'd left in this morning. She lay on a filthy-looking cot, her hair wrapped in a black-and-cream scarf and wearing a cream pants suit. Her eyes were closed, but she was clearly breathing. His eyes zeroed in on the rope that bound her wrists together and his stomach lurched sickeningly.

"What do you want?" Fear filled him—fear for Imani and how this could affect their unborn child.

"Twenty-five million dollars in large bills to be delivered to a place and at a time you will learn about tomorrow. Not before. We will contact you at noon with the details."

Twenty-five million seemed a paltry sum to request from a man with unfathomable wealth. Further, they'd kidnapped a queen. They'd taken a big risk, seemingly for no reason.

"And if I don't deliver as you request?" he asked.

"Then you will never see your queen again. And you will lose your heir."

Both sentences sent waves of shock through Wasim. How could this man—this stranger—possibly know that Imani was pregnant when she'd only told Wasim yesterday? Her pregnancy was to be kept quiet for now. Had this person seen the ultrasound she carried in her purse to surprise her Zambian family with, or had Imani said something to him? And how dare he threaten the two of them?

A new emotion replaced the fear. Anger.

Wasim straightened to his full, regal height. "Do you know who you are speaking to? I am your king. She is your queen."

"Yes, you are my king. But I have your queen. What will you do to get her back?"

"I will do whatever it takes to get her back. Everything in my infinite power," Wasim snarled. "I will get your money and deliver it to the place and at the time that you request. And you will deliver her to me safe and sound. No harm will come to her or my unborn child. If either of them is hurt in any way, pray that the authorities find you before I do. If there is a single scratch or bruise on Imani's body, or follicle of her hair removed because of your hands, I will rain down my wrath upon you and everyone you love—here and abroad. I will destroy you and everything you know and love. You will rue the day that you ever took from His Excellency King Wasim ibn Khalid al-Hassan. Your people will know my name and feel my wrath for *generations to come!*"

For tense seconds, there was silence on the line, and then it went dead.

Wasim glared at his head of security. "Get everyone in here. *Now!*"

THE SECOND SECURITY team discovered Imani's guards on the roadway to the airport. They sent video and photos of the area to Wasim. He saw the two vehicles with the flattened tires, as well as her limo. He saw the shattered glass inside and outside of the limo.

How frightened she must have been in that situation. Eight men—nine if he counted the driver—and still she had been taken hostage by a bunch of amateurs on horseback with handmade poison darts. It didn't matter to him that the captors were also armed. His guards were professionals and should have been able to handle them.

Wasim paced Imani's apartment. He'd come in here to feel closer to her. Her perfume idled in the air, and all the little touches that she'd brought to the apartment caught his eye—a bookshelf stocked with African classics and literature she'd read as a child and the tapestries that hung on the wall. The patterns showcased the artistic talent of the women whose products she promoted to help them achieve economic independence.

The ransom had already been counted and placed into sacks, and now they waited to hear from the kidnappers about when and where to deliver the funds so they could formulate a plan to arrest them as soon as they picked up the money. But Wasim was restless, and he couldn't simply wait. There had to be something he could do. He wandered into Imani's bedroom, looking for what he didn't know. Something, anything that could help him help her.

Then it dawned on him that she had been enthralled by the Australian's security location gadget. So enthralled that she had accepted his offer to beta test the technology. Was she wearing any jewelry that used one of Heath's devices? He distinctly remembered her wearing at least one piece that contained the tracking device because she had mentioned a glitch when her head of security had tried to find her with it on.

Wasim rushed to her jewelry closet on the far side of the room hidden behind a panel and entered the code. As soon as he stepped inside, the lights came on in the room. He rummaged through the drawers, lifting out bracelets and necklaces heavy with precious stones. There was so much—including newer pieces sitting next to heirlooms. How could he tell which one was missing—or if it was gone at all?

Wasim stopped. He had to slow down and think. Imani was organized. She would keep them separate. Frantically, he pulled open each draw and finally found what he was looking for. Several pieces in a drawer with Heath's business card resting on top of them. An opal bracelet, the matching necklace, and—the ring! The ring was gone.

Was she wearing it?

He whipped out the video of her lying on the dark cot and saw the ring on her hand. Yes!

But since the program was in beta, there were bugs. With encryption and other issues, it might not work at all. He didn't have time to work with his security team and hers to figure all this out. Every minute, every second counted while Imani and his child were out there somewhere. He'd have to go to the source.

He picked up the business card and called the handwritten number on the front, assuming it was a private line Heath had given to Imani to reach him directly.

"Hello?" The man's nasal voice sounded tired and a bit disoriented. There was a seven-hour time difference, and Wasim had probably woken him up.

He rushed through an explanation and emphasized how

important it was to keep everything he'd shared confidential. He ended with, "If you could get this program up and running by tomorrow morning and find her, I will pay you an obscene amount of money."

He named a figure and Heath gasped.

"I'll get everything up and running *tonight*," he promised.

27

I mani took the cup of water from the man who came in to check on her. This was the second time he'd been in here since she woke up from the poison they'd shot into her. Both times he'd been very kind, apologetic, and downright deferential. He had offered her food, which she declined because she simply didn't have an appetite.

She handed him back the cup. "Why am I here? What is it that you want?"

He refused to answer with a shake of his head and walked out without saying a word. The lock engaged with a loud click, and she blew out a frustrated breath.

Could her abduction be related to the conservative factions in the government who didn't want Wasim to marry her in the first place? The ones who thought his programs were too progressive and his actions reckless? Were they making demands in exchange for her release? Not knowing was driving her crazy.

Imani lowered onto her side in the dark room and curled on the cot with her back pressed against the brick wall. She wasn't cold, but that position made her feel protected. She deduced that she was somewhere in the older part of the country because of the design of the room, illuminated by the street light coming in the single window at the top of the far wall.

At least they'd removed the rope from her wrists. She placed a hand on her belly, thinking for a moment about the baby that grew inside her. Thinking about how excited she and Wasim had been the day before.

Did he know where she was? Would he come get her soon?

She had no idea what time it was or how long she had been there, but the stressful nature of her predicament had worn her out. Her eyes fluttered closed. She only hoped that she would not be there much longer. These men were kind now, but what would happen if they didn't get whatever it was they wanted?

She fell into an uneasy sleep, one filled with dreams of men on horseback, icy eyes, and stinging pain to the neck that knocked her unconscious.

A loud *boom* startled her awake. Her eyes flew open, and she held her breath as the entire building trembled. She heard yelling and gunshots. Then quiet.

Her eyes darted around the room. Natural light came through the window, so it must be morning. Just after dawn was what she assumed.

Tense, she strained her ears, listening for the next sounds to let her know what was going on.

Shouting.

Male voices.

Then, "Your Excellency, wait!"

Another voice, achingly familiar and filled with anxiety. "Imani!"

"Wasim?" she whispered.

As she sat up on the cot, the lock disengaged, and the door burst open. She instinctively shrank into the corner until she saw the person in the doorway. It *was* him! Wasim stood for a moment at the door, wearing the same clothes she'd seen him in when she left for the airport. His hair was uncombed, there were bags under his eyes, and yet he'd never been more beautiful to her.

"Wasim!" She whispered his name again as relief flooded through her.

He rushed over and dropped to his knees to the concrete floor. He pulled her into his arms and she clung to his neck.

Four men dressed in military gear and carrying guns piled into the room behind him. When they saw that only she and Wasim were in there, two remained and the other two darted out, probably going to find more of her captors.

"Are you hurt?" Wasim ran his hands carefully down her arms, checking for injury.

Imani shook her head. "I'm fine."

He took her hands and stared at the bruises the rope left on her wrists. "You *are* hurt," he said, voice grim, lips tight.

"They're just bruises. It's nothing."

"They are *not* nothing." Angry fire flared to life in his copper-brown eyes. There would be dire consequences for the men who'd taken her.

He stood and lifted her into his arms, holding her against his chest as if she were the most precious, delicate thing.

Imani had held strong the entire time, but cradled in Wasim's arms, she allowed herself to relax. In his comforting arms, all her fears disappeared and she became confident that everything would be okay now.

She didn't have to be strong anymore, and she clung to his neck and hid her face against his throat. A tear squeezed from between her eyelids as he marched with her out the door and she listened to him bark orders in Arabic.

She and her baby were fine. Wasim was here and their ordeal—though short-lived—was finally over.

Two doctors and a nurse waited at the palace when Imani arrived and examined her in the private clinic. After they confirmed she and the baby were fine, she took a long bath and soaked in warm water filled with oils that moisturized her skin and filled the room with scents that helped her relax.

Afterward, feeling normal enough to eat, she consumed a plate of eggs, toast, fruit, and several glasses of orange juice. Wasim watched her as she ate. He didn't speak. He simply stared.

Finally, she smiled at him. "I'm fine, and you need to get some rest."

"I don't know if I'll ever rest again," he said grimly, running his hands through his hair and rumpling the tresses into further disarray.

She reached across the table and covered his hand with hers. "You will. And you'll get back to work."

He flipped over his hand and clasped hers. "While you were taking your bath, we learned who was behind the kidnapping."

"You don't have to tell me. One or more of the members of the Parliament who disagreed with us getting married?"

He laughed bitterly. "I wish. Then this wouldn't be so hard."

"I don't understand..."

"This person needed money for a major project that they couldn't finance on their own, and unbeknownst to me, they had already burned bridges with other investors. That bit of information was kept quiet at his request because he is part of the royal family. In essence, he was over-leveraged, and dishonest about his capabilities. This was an act of desperation to get the funding he needed." He looked steadily at her, telepathically conveying the answer.

Her heart filled with dismay when she immediately guessed the culprit. "Farouk."

"Yes," Wasim said in a defeated voice.

His brother-in-law and close friend had orchestrated a kidnapping to finance his business deal and prop up his faltering business.

"What does this mean?" Imani asked.

"He must suffer the same justice as the others he convinced to do this with him. Men who were promised money, who saw this as an opportunity to elevate their status by improving their finances."

"But why me?"

"Because he knew I would do anything to get you back. Because he knew that you were the one thing I couldn't lose. My love, my life, my soul."

His words warmed her heart. "Where are the men now?"

"They've all been imprisoned and await trial and judgment."

She knew what judgment would be meted out. Like in her own country, bringing harm to any member of the royal family was a crime punishable by death.

"What about Yasmin?" she asked tentatively.

Wasim withdrew his hand. He shook his head. "She's not involved. I've already questioned her, and I believe her. She was completely shocked by his actions and devastated he would lie and go to such lengths to finance the deal."

"Are you certain you want to give him the same punishment?"

He looked her squarely in the eye. "The law is the law."

"But you are the ultimate authority. Think about Yasmin, Malak, and the new baby. Yes, he was wrong, and he should be punished, but I wasn't harmed."

"*He took you*," Wasim said, his eyes going wide. He obviously couldn't believe her stance on the matter, and neither could she.

But her concern wasn't for Farouk. She was worried about

his family and the families of the men who'd helped him. They'd all suffer and she hated that.

"What if he'd injured you beyond the bruises? What if he'd hurt our child?"

"But he didn't. Wasim, he's your brother-in-law, and Yasmin is your sister."

"And you are my wife and carry my child."

"And what if I forgive him? All of them?" Imani asked.

"That is your choice. It is not mine." Wasim lifted up her hand and kissed the inside of her bruised wrist. "This conversation is over. I have made my decision. We won't talk about their judgment anymore."

"Wasim—"

"This conversation is over, Imani," he said in a harder tone, all softness disappearing from his face. "I want you to rest and let me worry about what has to be done next. I've already contacted your family in Zamibia to let them know that you are back safely. The communication secretary will issue a statement about everything that happened, including those involved. There is nothing more for you to do."

He stood and walked out the door.

28

W asim sat on a raised dais in The Great Hall of Appeals with male scribes and secretaries on either side of him capturing the decisions made after each applicant came to plead their case.

A few weeks had passed since Imani had been found, and there were times when he still couldn't sleep through the night. He sometimes woke multiple times, gathering her closer during each instance, no matter how close she already was. He'd increased her security and her social secretary was now required to send a copy of her daily itinerary to his assistant and any changes, no matter how minor, had to be updated immediately. He could tell that his insistence on keeping track of her every move was endearing at first but now wore on Imani's nerves. He didn't care. She'd have to deal with his paranoia until he got back to normal.

The next person to enter The Great Hall of Appeals was unexpected.

Wasim tensed at the sight of his sister, barefoot, holding her newborn son in her arms. She wore a white shayla on her head and walked meekly toward him instead of with the proud stride of the princess she was. She'd chosen to come to him this way because he hadn't accepted any of her correspondence and had refused to meet with her about Farouk. He didn't want to listen to her plead the case of the man who'd jeopardized the life of his family and almost thrown the entire kingdom into chaos.

The past few weeks had taken a toll on them all, but her in particular. Her husband had been involved in the kidnapping and now sat in a prison cell, awaiting final justice.

She stopped in front of him and lowered to her knees on the cushioned bench below him. "Good morning Wasim, Your Excellency, King of Barrakesch."

His lips tightened in anger. Not at her, but at the position Farouk had forced them all into. Akmal had been devastated. Their younger siblings had been disappointed and disillusioned because they admired him and looked up to him as an older brother. Malak was confused about why he couldn't play with his father and hadn't seen him in a long time because Yasmin didn't want him to see his father behind bars. And Wasim himself grieved the loss of their friendship.

"Please state your name for the record," Wasim said. Yasmin did and then he asked, "Why have you come here today?"

"I've come to plead for leniency for my husband."

She gave his full name, the nature of the crime, and the expected judgment. She swallowed and then reminded Wasim of how long he'd known Farouk and knew his true heart. She pointed out that he was a member of the family and had simply gotten in over his head. At his core, he was a good man, generous and loved by many. She gave examples of his kindness and presented letters of thanks he'd received over the years from people to whom he'd given money, paid off bills, or given a job.

Finally, with tears in her eyes, Yasmin said, "Spare his life, please. If not for him, then for me and our children. We will carry the shame of his actions forever, but don't take him away from us—from them. We both know what it's like to lose a parent at a young age."

That last sentence sank deep into his heart. The sudden loss of their mother had devastated them both. Though they eventually recovered, he remembered the confusion he felt when his father explained that their mother was gone. That she would never sing to him again, stroke his hair, or shower him with affectionate kisses.

Then he remembered Imani's words to him the morning she was found. Her willingness to forgive and concern for his sister and her children while she should be concerned about herself after being the victim of a major crime.

Wasim's hand balled into a fist on his thigh. "I will spare his life."

Yasmin's shoulders collapsed and she closed her eyes.

"But he must leave Barrakesch for good."

Her eyes flew open. "Wasim, please..."

"That is non-negotiable." He hated the thought of depriving his nephews of their father, but he hated what Farouk had done even more. "He took the most important people in my life. Because of greed."

"Not greed. He—" She shut down immediately when his eyes narrowed in anger. They were siblings, but she owed him the respect of his position in The Great Hall of Appeals.

He continued. "They could have been hurt. Anything could have happened. Those were the longest hours of my life. I aged fifty years with worry and I still worry. He must be punished, and I am being very generous. This is my ruling."

That last sentence indicated the scribes should start recording.

"Within forty-eight hours, he must turn over all business property and holdings to the kingdom and leave the country, never to return. If he sets foot on Barrakeschi soil again for any reason, he will be executed. He should also keep track of *my* movements, because if I see him anywhere, in any country in the world—I will kill him. For the rest of his life, he should carry the knowledge that his life is worthless to me, and if I ever set eyes on him, he is a dead man. Is that ruling to your satisfaction?"

The question was rhetorical. No one had ever argued with a king on his ruling. Once you'd pleaded your case and the king gave an answer, that answer was final.

"Yes, Your Excellency," Yasmin said.

"Good. He should thank Allah that my heart has softened enough to spare his life. But I will never. Ever. Forgive him."

"I understand. Thank you."

Still cradling her youngest against her chest, Yasmin walked away with her head downcast.

Their relationship had been forever changed, and though he'd spared Farouk's life, she was effectively without a husband. Wasim knew she would remain here under his protection, where she was allowed to live the life of a princess that she was accustomed to.

There was no way her husband could provide for his family now, with no business assets and cast out of his country. He might move to neighboring Dubai or Saudi Arabia to remain close to his family so that the boys could have some kind of relationship with him.

Despite the catastrophic fallout, one good thing had come out of this trauma. The usual drivel that had spewed from the mouths of the conservative Parliament members had all but disappeared. They'd softened their rhetoric and denounced the kidnapping of the queen and the potential heir.

The horror of such an outrageous crime had shaken the kingdom, and her strength had endeared her in the people's hearts, particularly after seeing the bruised faces of her captors.

The bad part of this whole ordeal was the broken family left behind. Wasim, Akmal, and their younger brothers would step in to be father figures to Yasmin's sons, but that didn't change how broken their family would be for a while.

His heart hurt for his sister, and he grieved the loss of a man he not only considered a good friend, but a member of his family.

29

After talking with housekeeping about changes she wanted to make to the floral arrangements in the formal dining room, Imani took a cool shower, dressed, and went to Wasim's apartment. She found him in his bedroom, seated on the edge of the bed and focused on his phone.

She stood by the door. "Hi," she said.

"Hi. Everything okay?" he asked.

"I'm not sure."

He frowned. "What do you mean?"

She sensed he was about to go immediately into fix-it mode. "I'm wondering about us."

His frown deepened. "What's wrong with us?"

Imani walked over to where he sat and stood in front of him. "You haven't touched me since the incident."

"That's not true. I have touched you," Wasim said.

"Correct, you have touched me. You've held my hand. You've hugged me. You've cuddled with me in bed. But you haven't made love to me. Why?"

He shook his head as if the very idea was terrible. "I don't think it's a good idea."

Imani took his phone and set it on a table. Then she walked back over and straddled his lap and hooked her arms around his neck. Looking into his eyes, she brushed a lock of hair from his forehead. "Why not?"

"Would you believe I'm afraid?" he said quietly.

"You? Afraid?"

His jaw tightened as a hand smoothed down the curve of her spine. "I want you—believe me, I want you. But I'm afraid to traumatize you anymore."

How had she ever thought this man didn't care about her? His concern was so evident in the words he'd just spoken and in his actions on a daily basis. He was attentive and at times drove her crazy with his overprotectiveness and concern, but she'd rather have both of those things than his indifference.

"I'm not fragile, Wasim. I won't break, and I want you to make love to me. I miss that part of our relationship. I want us to get back to normal. I don't want what happened to change our marriage."

Enough had changed already. Her relationship with Yasmin was strained and probably would remain that way for some time. Her sister-in-law carried the shame of her husband's actions, and Imani did her best to ensure that Yasmin didn't feel as if she blamed her in any way for what had happened. She hoped that their relationship could go back to a semblance of what it used to be—a close friendship that regularly had them laughing together while also working as collaborators on charitable projects they both cared deeply about.

"Imani, you went through a traumatic experience. I don't want to be an insensitive brute and fling myself on top of you."

She held back a laugh, but he must have seen the amusement in her eyes because he arched an eyebrow at her.

"First of all, you're my husband, and you wouldn't be

flinging yourself on top of me. Besides, I want to make love to you. Haven't you been listening?" She nuzzled his neck and kissed his Adam's apple. "I miss you, Wasim, *habibi*. I miss your touch, and I need you."

His hands grasped her hips and pulled her tighter against him so she could feel his growing erection. "Are you sure you're ready?" he asked in a low voice.

His voice was so sexy when he talked like that, he could practically melt the panties off her. "Yes, I'm fine. You won't break me."

Imani pushed the hem of her abaya higher on her thighs and his hands found their way beneath the soft material. When he discovered she wasn't wearing underwear, his breathing caught and his eyes filled with lust.

"I want you," Imani whispered, tenderly kissing his lips. "Make love to me. As gentle or as rough as you want. I just need you."

Wasim tunneled his fingers into her hair at the base of her skull and seized her mouth. The kiss was instantly erotic, but slow and undemanding. He pried her lips apart with his tongue and the sweet invasion made her purr with pleasure. He took his time and gave her a long, drugging kiss and pulled back every now and again before reclaiming her mouth.

She rubbed her aching core against the hardness in his pants, and when he teased her with a careless swipe of his thumb along the crease of her hips, she shivered with the long unfulfilled need to be taken by him.

"Yes," Imani breathed, tilting her head back so his tongue could sweep the underside of her chin.

Wasim stood with her in his arms and placed her on her back on the bed. Then he made love to her in earnest.

She sighed happily as he nipped at her neck and squeezed her breasts. The nipples beaded against his palms and she arched into his hands. They hurriedly undressed and then their naked bodies fused together. Because of the anticipation of making love to him, Imani was so wet and aroused that she came almost instantly, trembling under the strength of his pumping hips. He climaxed soon afterward, squeezing her tight against his body and emptying with a groan to the side of her neck.

Later, Imani flung an arm across his chest and rested her head on his shoulder. Wasim's fingers moved in an arch along the back of her neck and scalp in a tender massage.

"Is Her Royal Highness, my queen, satisfied now?" he asked in an amused voice.

Imani sighed contentedly. "Yes. Very satisfied."

A ROYAL FRIENDSHIP THAT SPANS YEARS

The yacht owned by His Excellency King Wasim ibn Khalid al-Hassan was recently seen anchored in the Seychelles. The king, his wife Her Royal Highness Queen Imani Karunzika, and their son Crown Prince Hasib were all on board, taking a much-needed vacation. Also present on board were the king's best friend Crown Prince Kofi Francois Karunzika of Zamibia, his Great Wife Princess Dahlia Karunzika, and their children.

In two days, they will be joined by the king's other best friend, His Serene Highness Prince Andres Luis Vasquez Alamanzar II of the Principality of Estoria, his wife Her Royal Highness Princess Angela Renee Lipscomb de Vasquez, and their daughter.

The friendship between the three men spans almost fifteen years, starting when they were students at university together. As they grow their families and lead their countries, they continue to introduce progressive agendas that set an example for monarchies and governments around the globe. The world has its eyes on these young royals. We expect to see more great things from them as they move their nations forward through great leadership and hope for a better tomorrow, with their wives by their side.

Read all 3 books of the Royal Brides series:
Princess of Zamibia (Royal Brides #1), between Dahlia Sommers and Crown Prince Kofi Karunzika—a secret baby romance where the prince comes to claim his heir.

Princess of Estoria (Royal Brides #2), between Angela Lipscomb and Prince Andres Luis Vasquez Alamanzar II—inspired by current events.

Queen of Barrakesch (Royal Brides #3), between Imani Karunzika and Crown Prince Wasim al-Hassan—their engagement is fake but their love...isn't.

ALSO BY DELANEY DIAMOND

Royal Brides

- Princess of Zamibia
- Princess of Estoria
- Queen of Barrakesch

Quicksand

- A Powerful Attraction
- Without You
- Never Again

Brooks Family series

- A Passionate Love
- Passion Rekindled
- Do Over
- Wild Thoughts
- Two Nights in Paris
- Deeper Than Love

Love Unexpected series

- The Blind Date
- The Wrong Man
- An Unexpected Attraction
- The Right Time
- One of the Guys
- That Time in Venice

Johnson Family series

- Unforgettable
- Perfect
- Just Friends
- The Rules
- Good Behavior

Latin Men series

- The Arrangement
- Fight for Love
- Private Acts
- The Ultimate Merger
- Second Chances
- More Than a Mistress
- Undeniable
- Hot Latin Men: Vol. I (print anthology)
- Hot Latin Men: Vol. II (print anthology)

Hawthorne Family series

- The Temptation of a Good Man
- A Hard Man to Love
- Here Comes Trouble
- For Better or Worse
- Hawthorne Family Series: Vol. I (print anthology)
- Hawthorne Family Series: Vol. II (print anthology)

Bailar series (sweet/clean romance)

- Worth Waiting For

Stand Alones

- Still in Love
- Subordinate Position
- Heartbreak in Rio

Other

- Audiobooks
- Free Stories

ABOUT THE AUTHOR

Delaney Diamond is the USA Today Bestselling Author of sweet, sensual, passionate romance novels. Originally from the U.S. Virgin Islands, she now lives in Atlanta, Georgia. She reads romance novels, mysteries, thrillers, and a fair amount of nonfiction. When she's not busy reading or writing, she's in the kitchen trying out new recipes, dining at one of her favorite restaurants, or traveling to an interesting locale.

Enjoy free reads and the first chapter of all her novels on her website. Join her mailing list to get sneak peeks, notices of sale prices, and find out about new releases.

Join her mailing list
www.delaneydiamond.com

facebook.com/DelaneyDiamond
twitter.com/DelaneyDiamond
instagram.com/authordelaneydiamond
bookbub.com/authors/delaney-diamond
pinterest.com/delaneydiamond

Made in the USA
Middletown, DE
19 April 2020

90294283R00113